Death By Magic

A Josiah Reynolds Mystery
Book Fourteen

Abigail Keam

Worker Bee Press

Copyright © 2020 Abigail Keam
Print Edition

ALL RIGHTS RESERVED

No part of this book may be reproduced or transmitted
in any form without written permission of the author.

The book is not about you or your friends,
so don't go around town bragging about it.

Special thanks to Melanie Murphy.

ISBN 978 1 953478 00 9
721

Published in the USA by

Worker Bee Press
P.O. Box 485
Nicholasville, KY 40340

Books By Abigail Keam

Death By A HoneyBee I
Death By Drowning II
Death By Bridle III
Death By Bourbon IV
Death By Lotto V
Death By Chocolate VI
Death By Haunting VII
Death By Derby VIII
Death By Design IX
Death By Malice X
Death By Drama XI
Death By Stalking XII
Death By Deceit XIII
Death By Magic XIV
Death By Shock XV

The Mona Moon Mystery Series
Murder Under A Blue Moon I
Murder Under A Blood Moon II
Murder Under A Bad Moon III
Murder Under A Silver Moon IV
Murder Under A Wolf Moon V
Murder Under A Black Moon VI
Murder Under A Full Moon VII
Murder Under A New Moon VIII

Last Chance For Love Romance Series
Last Chance Motel I
Gasping For Air II
The Siren's Call III
Hard Landing IV
The Mermaid's Carol V

1

My name is Josiah Louise Reynolds. I am a bee-keeper and a widow. I limp with my left leg and wear a hearing aid tucked beneath my signature red hair worn over my ears. I am known for my sarcastic humor and sleuthing skills. I like to solve puzzles.

I have a farm which borders the Bluegrass Palisades. My beloved house, the Butterfly, hugs a cliff overlooking the Kentucky River. It is a modern cradle-to-the-grave concept house, made of local limestone, wood, concrete, and lots and lots of glass on the backside with a commanding view of the river.

However, I was not in the Butterfly, but at a social event at the stately, elegant mansion next door, which is called the Big House and belongs to Her Ladyship—Lady Elsmere. I was nursing a bourbon neat and sitting on an antique mohair wingback chair, while also nursing my throbbing left leg, when I looked up to see our bejeweled hostess, Lady Elsmere, hobble by and plop herself down in a matching chair next to me.

Lady Elsmere asked, "Aren't you going in?"

"I don't need a fortune teller shuffling the cards about my future. I'd rather not know if the next five years are going to be as crappy as the last five years. Why don't you have your fortune read?"

"I know my future. It's the grave. It's getting closer each day as I draw another one of those finite number of breaths I have left."

"Oh, put a cork in it," I said, taking a sip of outrageously expensive bourbon filched from June's private stock. I couldn't bear the thought of Lady Elsmere, aka June Webster from Monkey's Eyebrow, Kentucky dying. I wanted June to live forever, or at least until I crossed over to the other side of the River Jordan. How could I go on without that old biddy pestering me every day? I didn't want to try. I loved her.

"What a way to talk to me. You're such an ungrateful brat."

"Quit talking about dying. You've been riding this horse for over two months, and the poor creature is running out of steam."

"I feel death creeping up on me, Josiah. We need to discuss things."

I shot June an irritated look and was going to say something very rude when Franklin, who had just gotten his fortune told, popped out of the library with a grin on his face. "I'm going to be a bride," he gushed.

"Somebody had a good fortune," June said. "Tell us all about it."

Franklin pulled up a chair as someone else in the queue went inside the library. "Madam Lemore said I was going to be married within the next two years, and it was going to be with someone I already knew. I'm so excited."

"I wouldn't start buying a trousseau yet," I sniggered, taking another sip of my bourbon.

Franklin slapped my knee in aggravation. "Party pooper. Hey, where's your sense of fun? Just sour and dour is all I get from you anymore." He made a face at me. "This is supposed to be a party. Let's have fun!"

June chimed in. "Yes, Josiah. You are putting a damper on my fundraiser. People are staring."

I managed a smile and out of the corner of my mouth, hissed, "My leg hurts. I want to go home to rest."

June hissed back, "You can rest in the grave. Now go work the room, and try not to make too many enemies." She turned to Franklin. "Sweet boy, will you escort me? I feel more secure with someone at my elbow as I greet my guests."

"I get it. You want some arm candy. Can do, Lady Elsmere." Franklin jumped up and offered June his arm.

As they were walking away, I heard Franklin ask June if he could try on her diamond and ruby tiara that she was wearing to which she briskly replied, "NO!"

I chuckled. Some things never change. June and

Franklin were right. I *was* being a party pooper. I got up and mingled with friends, making an effort to look interested listening to their tales of grandchildren, stock options, and doctor appointments. What I wouldn't give for a good discussion on political art in the twentieth century or the symbolism of Kentucky folk art carvings. I checked out the jewelry trunk sale, the silent auction room, and the Kentucky Derby hat sale. A percentage of the sales went to support retired Thoroughbred horses. It was no secret most owners got rid of their horses after their monetary value expired. Mature mares and stallions were thrown onto the heap, so to speak. Many were sold out of the country and slaughtered for their meat. Both June and I had spoken out against the overbreeding of Thorough-breds, but to no avail. There was too much money to be made by mating champion studs with broodmares.

June decided to host a charity party raising money for the upkeep of retired horses and put pressure on horse owners to have an effective retirement plan for horses under their care. I had already rescued two racehorses, but I went to the adoption table, signing up to take another one. I had enough land.

"I signed up for one, too," a voice floated over my head.

I put the pen down and turned around. "Good for you," I said, looking up at a tall man with a slight tan, graying blonde hair, regular features, and a deep

Southern accent. "What are you going to do with your Thoroughbred?"

"I'm going to ride him for pleasure."

I bit my lip. Thoroughbreds, trained as racers, did not make good pleasure horses. They were called hot bloods for a reason as their temperaments were rather feisty, but I guessed this man would learn it on his own.

The genteel gent held out his hand. "My name is Rutherford Robert Lee."

I shook it. "Let me guess. You are from the Deep South."

He laughed. "How could you tell? Was it my name or my accent that gave me away? I hail from Louisiana."

"My name is Josiah Reynolds. I'm Kentucky born and bred."

"Your accent isn't Kentucky."

"I'm from northern Kentucky. We have a more midwestern accent."

"Nice to meet you, Josiah from Kentucky."

"Rutherford Robert Lee from Louisiana, what brings you here?"

Lee smiled, showing off a gap-toothed grin. "I'm looking to get into the Standardbred business."

"Trotters?"

"Pacers."

I wasn't versed enough in the difference between trotters and pacers as they were the same to me, so I changed the subject. "Are you investing into a syndicate?"

"I am going into business alone."

"Oh, my, you are ambitious, Mr. Lee."

"Call me Rudy. All my friends do."

"Okay, Rudy. What does going into business 'alone' mean?"

"I'm going to buy my own farm here and pull up stakes from Louisiana. Too many hurricanes for me."

"You know Kentucky is known for its tornadoes in the spring."

"I'd rather face a thundercloud which passes by in seconds than a hurricane that lasts for hours."

"Tornadoes are a little more treacherous than that, but have it your own way." I thought for a moment. "You know, Mr. Lee."

"Rudy."

"Yes, Rudy, sorry. Instead of buying a horse farm, why don't you lease one? That way, if things don't turn out the way you plan, you won't be stuck with the property or the taxes."

"Hmm. Never thought of that. You got a farm in mind, Josiah from Caintuck?"

"I know of a farm on the northwest side of Lexington. Closer to Versailles on old Frankfort Pike. Barns and paddocks have been renovated. Great pastures with lots of clean water. A stream runs through the entire farm. Sturdy fences."

"Does it have a training track?"

"Yes, but it hasn't been renovated yet. It's still clogged with weeds, but the farm next door has one, and I'm sure they would let you use it."

"Would I have to transport the horses with a trailer to the farm next door? That's a lot of trouble. There's a lot of equipment needed for harness racing, not to mention the sulky. I'd like to harness the horse to the sulky and walk him over to the track to train."

"If there is not an adjacent gate between the two properties, I'm sure one can be installed. I can't vouch for the length of the course, though. I know Thoroughbred and Standardbred courses are different. The farm is owned by Hunter Wickliffe, and he has been looking for a leasee. In fact, his brother, Franklin, is escorting Lady Elsmere about." I swung my head around looking for them.

"Is there a house on the farm?"

"Yes, Wickliffe Manor, but it is occupied by Hunter Wickliffe. I think only the pastures and the barns are available."

"Is Mr. Wickliffe here today?"

"It's Dr. Wickliffe." I turned back. "He is out of town on business, but he'll be back next week. Let me get you Franklin for further information. I don't know all of the details." I started to search for Franklin, but Rudy grabbed my arm.

I glared angrily at the big paw encircling my wrist.

Rudy pulled back immediately. "Forgive me for my rudeness, but I came here to enjoy myself. Not talk business."

I guess my face displayed the negativity I was feeling because Rudy continued, "Josiah, I'm so sorry. I seem to have made a bad first impression. Can we start over, please?"

"I understand. Please excuse me, Mr. Lee. I see someone I know." I walked away. Was I making a big deal out of nothing? Probably, but I don't like men putting their hands on me, especially after what happened to me in the past. There was no need of Rudy Lee to grab my arm.

Perhaps if I had been more assertive with men from my youth, I wouldn't have had a husband cheat me out of money or a deranged cop pull me off a cliff. Those two things make me a little testy concerning the male gender. My rule of thumb is if a man says the sky is blue, better stick your head out a window and see for yourself. Not that a woman can't be an utter nightmare, but I've rarely had a woman point a gun at me. Oh, wait a minute. I have had women point guns at me. Scratch that. Let's say the entire human race is full of manure and leave it at that.

Most of the guests were herded out to the paddocks to view retired racehorses who needed a home. June made an impassioned plea that horse owners need to be responsible, instead of using horses up and then throwing them away like garbage. She made a good case the world was watching how the racing business treated horses, and the inhumane treatment in the horse business world would no longer be tolerated by the public if the sport of kings was to last.

I moseyed into the kitchen where the catering staff was running about filling empty trays with bite-sized eclairs, lemon tarts, and poppy seed muffins. I grabbed a flute of champagne and some éclairs only to steal away to the main foyer where I plopped down in the mohair wingback chair by the library again. Since everyone was outside, I could enjoy my booty without someone interrupting me while I chewed on an éclair.

Suddenly, the door to the library flew open. Rudy stumbled into the foyer, mopping his sweating forehead with a silk handkerchief and grabbing his left arm while looking confused. I recognized the signs of angina and jumped up. "Rudy, take my seat. Do you have any pills?"

"In my pocket."

I rummaged through his coat pockets, finding a small bottle of nitroglycerine. After putting a small white pill under his tongue, I handed him a bottle of water from a table. "Feel better?"

"Yes, thank you." He wiped his brow again.

"There are several doctors here. Let me get one."

"Not necessary. Nothing they can do."

"I'm going to call an ambulance."

Rudy grabbed my hand.

Why was he always grabbing me? I shook him loose.

Seeing my chagrin at his touching me again, Rudy smiled as he loosened his tie. "I keep making the same mistakes with you."

"I don't like being touched by strangers."

"Obviously."

"Can we discuss my foibles later? You need medical attention."

Rudy shook his head. "Nothing anyone can fix. That's why I'm here. To spend my last days living my fantasy. I've always loved Standardbreds and harness racing."

"May I sit with you until you feel better?"

"I would like nothing better, Josiah."

I unbuttoned his shirt collar.

Rudy kidded, "Josiah, we haven't even had dinner yet, and you start taking liberties with me."

"I have experience with people having cardiac episodes."

"How did you know I had heart disease?"

I thought that an odd question. Perhaps Rudy was confused. "I think the nitroglycerine tablets were a clue. Also, my husband had it. I recognized the look."

"Sorry for your loss."

"I'm not. He was a skunk."

Rudy tried to chuckle, but winced instead.

"I think you need to go to an emergency room and get checked out."

He shook his head. "Your help has been enough. As soon as I get my wind back, I'm going home to rest."

"Did you come with a plus one?"

"I came alone."

"I'll get one of Charles' grandsons to drive you home. I'll follow so I can bring him back."

"Who is Charles?"

"Lady Elsmere's heir." I looked around. "He must be outside with the guests on the patio. I'll fetch him. You shouldn't drive home by yourself."

"I'll call a cab. I don't want anyone to bother with this. I'll pick up my car tomorrow."

As luck would have it, Franklin wandered into the foyer wearing June's diamond tiara.

"Franklin, just the person I wanted to see."

"Yeeessss?"

"This is Rudy Lee. He is feeling a bit under the weather. I was wondering if you could drive him home now."

Franklin scrunched up his nose. I could tell he didn't want to leave the party.

I hurried to add, "Mr. Lee is looking for a horse farm to lease. He's interested in pacers."

"Ah, Standardbreds. Nice breed." Franklin's face lit up. "My brother has a farm and is looking for someone to lease it. Perhaps I could show it to you."

"Maybe later this week. I'm not feeling up to it right now."

"Surely. My brother is out-of-town currently, but I could set something up. Never hurts to look, eh?"

I swiped June's tiara off Franklin's head. "I'm sure Lady Elsmere will be looking for this." It was an unspoken rule that we always addressed June as Lady Elsmere in public.

Franklin grimaced. "Shoot, Josiah. You always spoil my fun. I wish Lady Elsmere would just give it to me. She knows I love it."

"Where in the world would you wear it?"

Franklin waved my concerns away about the tiara and said to Rudy, "I'll tell the valet to get my car. It will just be just a moment or two." He rushed off to gather his car while I helped Rudy to his feet.

As Rudy and I slowly walked to the front portico where Franklin's car would be waiting, I asked, "Do you know what set off this episode?"

"I went to see the fortune teller. I thought it would be a bit of fun."

"Is that what threw you into a tizzy?"

Rudy turned toward me. "She said I was going to murder someone, and then be murdered myself. I usually don't give credence to such nonsense, but she knew so much about me—details about my personal life most people don't know. She completely threw me.

When she predicted the murders, my chest started to tighten. I knew I needed to get away from her, but I was having trouble breathing. Ugly things kept spilling from her mouth, so I fled. I feel discombobulated even now." He glanced furtively at the library door and shuddered.

"Wow! That's a bummer. Fortune tellers at parties usually give out happy fortunes. Whom are you supposed to kill?"

With absolute sincerity, Rudy said, "You!"

2

I knocked on the library door and hearing no reply, I opened the heavy carved wooden door and peeked around it. "Hello?"

A woman with a pixie-cut blonde hair, chic-looking Italian black eyewear, a conservative gray dress with long sleeves, pale beige manicure, and expensive Swarovski jewelry sat in a chair near the fireplace. She was not at all what I was expecting. The woman looked as though she was a high-powered lawyer or an executive—not a person in the magic trade, pushing charms and looking into crystal balls.

"Are you busy?" I asked.

"I've been expecting you, Mrs. Reynolds." She waved her hand at the seat in front of her. "Please, be seated."

"How do you know my name? I don't believe I've met you."

She raised a finger to her temple and tapped it. "I just know things. You were expecting a shriveled-up, old woman wearing a babushka resembling the Russian actress Maria Ouspenskaya from *The Wolf Man*. Though a man be pure in heart and says his prayers at night.'"

I finished the rest of the quote. "'May become a wolf when the wolfsbane blooms, and the autumn moon is bright.'" I shot her a suspicious look. "Why did you say that quote?"

"I know you are a cinephile, and this poem is one of your favorites from *The Wolf Man*."

"Not many people know who Maria Ouspenskaya is anymore."

"True."

My hackles were up now. Something was not kosher with this lady. How did she know I loved Maria Ouspenskaya? Still, I braved on. "Most people know I love old movies. Not hard to find out. What's your game, lady?"

"No game. Glimpses of a person's life come to me. I guess you could say it's magic."

I could no longer hide my distrust. "Doesn't fill me with confidence you yakking about me with my friends. I think you're running a clever con."

"You are experiencing trouble with your kidneys."

I gasped. "Who have you been talking to?"

"No one, because you haven't told anyone. You shouldn't keep your daughter in the dark for your time is running out."

"If I'm going south because of my kidneys, why does it matter if Rudy Lee murders me then?"

The fortune teller leaned back in her chair and said nothing, clasping her hands.

"You want to tell me about that?"

"The future is never fixed. I tell you what is most probably the future. It is up to you to change it."

"No predestination?"

The fortune teller smiled. "We all have free will, but we all follow patterns of predictable behavior which lead to our downfall." She scooted her chair closer to mine and reached out to me. "I must see if your future matches Mr. Lee's. Let me hold your hand."

I pulled back. "No way that's going to happen. Think again."

"Then let me touch something personal belonging to you."

"Let's do this. I ask questions and you answer. Why did you tell Rudy Lee that he was going to kill me?"

The woman gave a patronizing smile as if she were addressing a senile, old aunt. "I see death all around you. You attract it wherever you go like a moth to the flame. Death either proceeds or greets you upon your arrival. Your aura is dark and flickers as your life energy is drained bit by bit. You are on a downward spiral both spiritually and physically."

"You want to know what I see? A big right hook in the old eyeball if you don't answer my questions."

"You are indeed a violent person, Josiah Reynolds. This will lead to your eventual demise."

"I'm beginning to think you are correct. I usually don't hit women, but I can make an exception in your case." The truth is I don't have the energy to hit anyone, let alone this young chick who could bounce me on my fanny. I just like to sound tough.

"I told Mr. Lee to beware. He is in terrible danger and to be cautious of you as the two of you draw negative energy from each other."

"Did you use the word *murder* with Mr. Lee? It is a simple question—yes or no."

The fortune teller closed her eyes and pinched her nose as though thinking back. "I may have said violence would follow you both when together."

"Did you tell Rudy Lee that he was going to kill me?"

"What is inevitable for Mr. Lee will be."

"Can't you answer a simple question?"

"I answered to what I see. Let me speak to *your* future. Give me your hand."

"Ah, phony baloney. I can see I am wasting my time. Mr. Lee had a heart episode due to your little talk with him. I can see you won't tell me the truth, but you flustered him so much he had a spell. Think about that next time you tell someone they are going to be murdered."

"And murder as well."

"So now we come to the crux of what was said."

"Stay away from Mr. Lee, Josiah Reynolds. It is my duty to warn you both. The stars are not aligned in your favor."

"Jumping Jehoshaphat! Lady, you are something. This conversation is too crazy, even for me." As I was leaving the room, the fortune teller jumped up. "He touched you, didn't he?"

I turned. "Maybe."

"That's how I knew you would be his victim. I read his palm and, as I touched him, I saw flashes of the future. I see things with my hands. It's how I knew about you." She stretched out her arm, pointing her index finger at me. "Mr. Lee will try to kill you. You've been warned."

I shook my head. "It's a little early for Halloween. See ya in the fall." I closed the library door silently only to bump into someone waiting to see the fortune teller. "Good luck. You'll need it," I said to the guest.

"How was your fortune?" the guest asked.

"Unbelievable."

"That good, huh? I hear she is one of the best and has an enormous following. I can't wait for her to read my fortune. Wish me good fortune, honey." The guest bravely knocked on the door and entered.

I decided enough was enough. Sneaking out through the back French doors leading out from the breakfast room, I walked out into the evening, heading for the Butterfly, only to find myself looking over my shoulder. I was so nervous, I almost jumped out of my shoes when a mockingbird flew out of a bush. I didn't like the thought of an empty house and checked all the windows and double locked the doors as soon as I got home. Mr. Lee wasn't the only one perturbed after talking with the fortune teller.

It suddenly dawned on me that I didn't even know the fortune teller's first name or if Lemore was really her last name. I really am a lousy sleuth. Miss Marple would be so ashamed of me.

3

I barged into June's room where she was having breakfast and jumped on the bed, stealing a piece of buttered toast.

"Help yourself," June said, sarcastically. She pushed the kitchen button on her house phone. "Bess, Jo just landed in my bed and is eating my breakfast. Can you have one of the lads bring up her own breakfast tray?"

"And a pot of hot tea," I yelled.

June clasped the phone to her bosom. "Bess wants to know what type of tea."

I shrugged. "I don't care."

Exasperated, June said into the phone, "Did you hear that? Thank you, Bess. Yes, I know she's a nuisance, but what can we do?" She put the receiver into its cradle.

"A nuisance am I?"

"Most assuredly."

"Well, then, I guess you don't want to hear about Rudy Lee having a heart episode in your foyer after speaking with that dreadful fortune teller you hired."

June was about to take a sip of her coffee when she put the cup down. "What did you say?"

I got up off the bed and started for the door. "No. No. I'm a pest. You shan't be bothered with me today."

"Come back here, you detestable woman."

I jumped back on the bed. "May I have that scrumptious cheese Danish?"

"Help yourself, but only if you spill about Rutherford Robert Lee."

"How do you know him?"

"I knew his father way back. Their money comes from sugar, and the Lee family was one of the largest growers of it."

"Did you know his father in the biblical sense?"

"Is that all you think about?"

"No, it is all you think about, which is unseemly for a lady of your advanced age."

June sniffed. "I don't know what you mean."

"I mean this side of the bed looks mussed."

"I'll scoot over so you won't be defiled by some man's cooties."

"Please do," I said. "I don't know how you lure men into the holy of holies."

"Money. Lots and lots of money," June replied, grinning.

"You mean you pay for sex?"

"It's not my looks that gets men in my bed anymore. I know I'm a wrinkled prune. It's the possibility of favors down the line. A phone call here. A discreet whisper into the ear of a bank manager for a substantial loan. You see where this is going."

I was stunned as this was a new development in June's behavior. "You're pimping out your resources for a little kissy face."

"Don't look at me like that. You think being a woman is going to get easier as you get older? People stop looking at a woman after fifty. You become invisible, so if I use my money and power to get some romantic attention, who are you to judge? I use what I have. A gal gets lonely at night."

"Another gloom and doom prediction of what my life will become. Thanks for the uplifting speech."

"It is what it is."

"He's not in the bathroom, is he?"

"Left hours ago. Before the sunrise. I guess he didn't want to see my ancient face in the bright light of day."

We both looked at each other and laughed until we heard a knock on the door, and Bess entered with a breakfast tray.

I stretched out on the bed as Bess placed the tray in my lap. "Thank you, Bess."

"This isn't going to become a regular thing, is it, Josiah? I have lots to do before lunch, and I don't want to be traipsing up and down the stairs because of you."

"Ouch, Bess. I didn't know I was putting you out."

"It's not you so much as that horse-sized mutt stationed downstairs. Baby has already gone through my turkey and is now working on the baloney lunch meat. He is underfoot."

I felt embarrassed. I should have kept a closer eye on my English Mastiff. "Send him up here, Bess. Very sorry."

"Don't you feed that dog?"

"Constantly."

"Keep him away from me today. I'm making pickles and don't want Baby in my way."

"Yes, ma'am."

Bess left the door open, and I heard her call for Baby from the top of the stairs. There was a sound of my dog whining as he clomped upstairs while Bess went downstairs in the elevator, which squeaked down to the first floor.

"BABY!" I yelled. "I'm up here." I heard the soft thudding of Baby's paws and knew he would find me. He eventually sniffed my whereabouts and plunked his huge head on the bed. I gave Baby some bacon and told him to lie in the corner. Of course, he padded into June's powder room and climbed into the bathtub to take a snooze. "Where did we leave off?" I asked, cutting into my buttermilk pancakes.

"You said Rudy Lee became ill yesterday."

"You were going to tell me how well you knew Rudy Lee's father."

"A few business deals. That's all. Now tell me what's going on."

I related my initial conversation with Lee and subsequent meeting with him after his talk with the fortune teller.

"She told Rudy that he was going to murder you and then, in turn, he was going to be murdered?"

"That's what he claimed."

"And he wasn't teasing? Perhaps he was playing a trick on you because you brushed him off."

"I don't think so. The man really seemed to be in jeopardy. As I was unbuttoning his collar, I felt his heart. It was beating a mile a minute. His face was beet red and he was struggling to breathe. I don't know if it was a full grade heart attack, but it was some kind of an episode."

"What did Lettie Lemore say to you?"

"That's her name? Lettie?"

"Lettie Lemore. She is from Louisville and has a huge following. There is even talk of a radio talk show in the works."

"I don't see how that could happen. She claimed she needed to touch in order to make a connection."

"I'm just telling you what I have heard," June said. "Lemore has a website. Charles checked her out and thought she was legit."

Charles had been June's butler, but now was her heir and ran her estate. Bess was his daughter and ran the Big House for June. She was also a fabulous cook. Cooking was an art form with Bess. I never turned down any of her meals. It was an honor to eat whatever she fried, baked, canned, roasted, flambéed, pickled, poached, stewed, shelled, toasted, barbequed, crocked, cured, or smoked.

June continued, "I thought she would be fun for my guests. I had no idea such a kerfuffle would occur. I must call Rudy and apologize."

"What are you going to do about Lettie Lemore?"

"What should I do?"

"She threatened Rudy and me."

"I guess it never occurred to you to take her advice and stay away from Rudy Lee."

"Oh, my gawd, you don't believe Lemore's prattle?"

"What if Lemore does have a gift and the warning is on the level? You do attract a lot of dead bodies, Jo. What if it's your turn?"

"What if the moon is made of cheese, and there is a pot of gold at the end of the rainbow?"

"No need to get snotty."

"Lemore knew things about me she shouldn't have known. Someone has been feeding her information."

"Like who?"

"How about Brannon's mistress, Ellen Boudreaux?" Brannon was my husband who cheated on me with a woman half my age.

June scoffed. "Why?"

"Because she's a petty husband-stealer, who hates me."

"Like you hate her? Jo, you've gotten back on your feet financially. The Butterfly is raking in money now. Asa is doing well. You have a nice boyfriend. Why go down this path with Ellen? Don't rock the boat with crazy accusations. No good can come of it."

I had to admit June was right. "There are only two ways of looking at this. Either Lettie Lemore is the real deal and she can see into the future, or someone is setting Rudy and me up for a fall."

"I think the thing is for Charles to interview the staff and see if anyone had come sniffing around about you."

"That would be a good start. I'll call Franklin and see if he has any dope on Rudy."

"You need help with this."

I knew June was right again. I needed answers fast, but I couldn't bring myself to ask anyone for help. Every time I did go to someone for help, they got hurt.

I decided this was on me.

4

I didn't call anyone. Instead, I went to work. At six in the morning, I arrived at my booth site at the farmers market. I set up my table with the help of my booth neighbor. Once I had my umbrella installed and my chair ready, I pulled out honey from storage boxes kept in the car. Due to the still cold nights, some honey was beginning to crystallize. I put those bottles under the table, but put out a sign that crystallized honey was available. Most of the world eats crystallized honey, but Americans won't touch it as they think the honey is bad. Honey never goes bad unless it ferments. It had taken many years to educate my customers to put their crystallizing jar of honey in the sun so it would re-liquefy or they could eat it as is. Still, many would throw the bottle away and complain next time they saw me, but they would buy more honey from me.

It takes me an hour to set up. I had thirty bottles of Black Locust honey to sell. Pure locust honey from the blossoms of the Black Locust tree looks like water. It is clear, thin, and very sweet. It is my most expensive honey as the trees bloom in spring, and the hives have to be harvested immediately before the bees bring nectar from other spring plants into the hives. Besides being labor intensive to harvest, it was becoming rarer as people were cutting down Black Locust trees due to their propensity to become damaged during storms. People considered them "trash" trees.

In addition, I had Clover honey from last year. This honey is golden and mild tasting. I also had Buckwheat honey, which is almost black and has a strong taste. I find Buckwheat bitter tasting, but many people buy it because it has the most antioxidant properties of any U.S. honey. I sow white Dutch clover seeds in the pastures for the Clover honey, and I plant half an acre of Buckwheat as it is a cover crop. I consider the rest of my honey Wild as the nectar comes strictly from Mother Nature herself without any help from me.

By seven o'clock, I had customers. By eleven, the Locust honey was sold out and I was pulling out the last of my bottles from the back of my Prius.

"Let me help you with that box, Josiah."

I looked up to see my old pal, Officer Kelly, grinning broadly at me. He grabbed the box from me and carried it over to my table.

"I'm so happy to see you."

"I know it's been a while." Kelly gave me a big grin.

"Did you get my note congratulating you for capturing that bank robber?"

"I did. Thank you."

"I thought you worked as a detective in homicide now, so what were you doing nabbing a gun-toting bank robber?"

"I happened to be in the bank withdrawing money." Kelly laughed loudly. His auburn hair fluttered a bit in the breeze.

I detected bitterness in his laugh. "Was it really like *Dirty Harry*? I read in the paper you received another commendation."

He turned to face me. "I did. You wanna know the truth?"

"Sure."

"The guy was an easy collar. He was robbing the bank because his daughter had leukemia, and he had no health insurance. He's now in jail, and a little girl doesn't have her father. The mother barely sees her daughter because she's now working two jobs trying to pay for her daughter's medical care. This country stinks when it comes to health care. Really stinks. You know who goes to see her? My kids and me, that's who."

I could tell Kelly felt terrible about arresting the father, but then again, the man was robbing a bank. That's a big no-no in my book, but people do desperate things in desperate times. Who was I to judge after all the rotten things I had done? I quickly thought of the stash of illegal pain killers stashed away in my bedroom.

I know I'm a hypocrite. You don't need to point a finger at me. "Why don't you start a virtual fundraising account for the little girl?"

"What's that?"

"Internet sites where you can set up an account to ask people to contribute money for a particular cause. People like helping other people, and this is a sob story if ever I heard one."

Kelly's face brightened. "That's a great idea." He grabbed me, kissing on my forehead.

I tried not to flinch at his touch. My aversion to touch was becoming troublesome. Maybe I should see a professional about it. "Is that why you came to see me?"

"Yeah. I was feeling pretty crummy about pinching the guy. I knew you would make me feel better."

"Glad I could help, but you were doing your job, Kelly. We can't have people going around and holding up banks."

He nodded. "I know. I know, but the things I see every day either rip my heart out or disgust me to no end. There's no even keel with this job."

"If you want to feel like you're walking on a cloud, get Shaneika Mary Todd to be this guy's lawyer. Get her to do it pro bono."

"I've already asked her. She said she wasn't a charitable institution."

I chuckled. "I'm sure she will change her mind in

time. Let her think on it."

"Enough about me. What's going on with you?"

"Funny you should ask." I told him about my bizarre experience with Lettie Lemore and Rudy Lee.

"It's a strange tale for sure, Josiah," Kelly said after listening to my story.

"Have you heard anything about this Lettie Lemore?"

"I've heard of her. Some of the bigwigs in the racing business consult her."

"And?"

"Nothing out of the ordinary. She's based in Louisville. I can ask some of my contacts on the Louisville police force about her."

"Can't you look her up on your police computer? She might have a record."

He shook his head. "We are very strict about using our computer files unless a person is suspected of something. No can do. Asking around is the only thing I can do at this point."

"But we're talking about a possible murder."

"Are we? Or are we discussing a fake fortune teller spewing nonsense for who knows what purpose?"

"Can't someone at least interview Lettie Lemore?"

"Since you're standing here shooting the breeze with me, I'd say no crime was committed."

"How about fraud?"

Kelly shot me another one of his cheesy grins. "I'll

have to reserve judgment on that. Of course, if you turn up dead, then no fraud was committed."

"This isn't funny. I have a bad feeling about this." I was frustrated no one was taking Lettie Lemore seriously.

"Let me ask around, and we'll take it from there."

"Okay."

Kelly kissed me on the cheek and left.

I watched Detective Kelly leave.

Where's a cop when you need one?

5

After making a nice little bundle of cash, I packed up and headed toward Hunter's farm. He had called the night before and said he was back in town. I excitedly drove down Old Frankfort Pike and turned onto the driveway past the stone guard house. Hunter had left the gates open for me. Seeing his jalopy near the main barn, I turned in.

Hunter came out of the barn, looking fit in his tight jeans, cowboy boots, and a cotton work shirt with the sleeves rolled up at the elbows. The two top buttons of the shirt were unbuttoned exposing glistening skin and a tuft of dark chest hair. He hadn't shaved, and his face sported a faint shadow beard. I must confess my heart skipped a beat or two. Oh Lordy, how did this broken gal lasso someone like Hunter Wickliffe!

I got out and leaned against my car. "Howdy, stranger."

Smiling, Hunter came over and gave me a peck on the cheek.

Cheek? Nothing doing. I grabbed the front of his shirt and pulled Hunter to me, giving him a passionate kiss on the lips. Hunter smelled of sweat, expensive cologne, and horses.

"Hey, what gives?" Hunter said, pulling away. He seemed both pleased and embarrassed, wiping my lipstick from his lips.

"Just glad to see you, that's all." I grabbed him again. "Come back here. I'm not done."

Hunter leaned near my bad ear with the hearing aid and whispered, "Later. I've got someone in the barn."

I let go of his shirt. "Yeah, about that. I want to talk to you about leasing your farm. Something really strange happened while you were gone."

Hunter couldn't wait to tell me and cut in. "I want to thank you by taking you out to a fancy dinner tonight."

"Thank me for what?"

"Helping me lease my farm."

My heart skipped a beat again, but not for my sexy boyfriend. "Hunter, what have you done?"

"Hello, Josiah. Small world."

I swirled around to see Rutherford Robert Lee standing in front of the barn. "Thanks for giving me a heads-up about Wickliffe Farm. It's perfect for my needs," Rudy said.

"That was quick work on your part, Rudy, especially since you were so worried about Lettie Lemore's dire prediction."

"I thought about it and came to my senses. It's complete bunk. I called Franklin for an appointment, and once I saw Wickliffe Manor, decided I couldn't pass up such a great opportunity."

Hunter laughed. "In fact, Rudy's been twisting my arm to sell Wickliffe Manor to him."

"Perhaps it's you he's going to murder," I said, "but I might beat him to it." I was not happy, and I'm sure my body language conveyed my unhappiness to the two men.

"Huh?" Hunter said. "What's this?"

"Did Rudy tell you a fortune teller from Lady Elsmere's party prophesied that Rudy was going to murder me and then someone else was going to murder him?"

"What are you two yammering about?" Hunter demanded, looking back and forth between Rudy and myself.

"I'm afraid there was a misunderstanding at Lady Elsmere's party," Rudy said, taken aback. "A fortune teller at the fundraiser said I was going to murder someone."

"Me specifically," I said.

"Yes," Rudy concurred. "And then I was to be murdered myself. Complete rubbish. I don't know why I let it upset me so."

Hunter asked, "Did this soothsayer explain why you were going to kill Josiah?"

Rudy shook his head. "Before that day, I had never met this good lady."

Hunter slumped against my car and thought for a moment. Finally, he said, "Considering this new information, perhaps it would be better if you leased another farm, Rudy."

Rudy said, "No way. The contract is signed, and I expect you to live up to the agreement."

"Josiah is my special friend, and I will not put her in harm's way, even if based on such an outrageous story."

Rudy dug in his heels. "I intend to stay. If you push this, I'll sue."

Hunter's brow knotted together. He didn't like being threatened. "Now, look here."

"Boys. Boys!" I interrupted. "Let's compromise. Hunter, you need a tenant. Rudy, you need a place to train your horses. I'm the problem here. I just won't come around. Rudy can't kill me if he never sees me."

Hunter sputtered, "I can't believe we are having such a ridiculous conversation."

I said, "Rudy, let's agree to give each other a wide berth if we do see each other. Don't even wave or say hello. We'll just ignore each other's presence."

"Sounds like a plan to me," Rudy said.

Hunter looked worried while thrusting his hands in his jeans pockets. "I don't know. This whole thing sounds fishy."

Rudy pulled out his checkbook from his pants pocket and wrote a check. "I don't want any hard feelings between us, Hunter. This is the rent for the next six months. After six months, we'll reassess this arrangement. If everything has gone well, and nobody ends up dead, I'll write a check for the next six months. If not, I'll leave."

I peeked at the check. It was a high five figures. "Hunter, take the check. You can repair the water line and the roof for Wickliffe Manor."

"Are you sure, Josiah?"

I could tell he still had doubts. "Go ahead, Hunter. It's fine. You can't pass up this opportunity."

Hunter reluctantly took the check and shook hands with Rudy. "Six months then, Rudy. I'm going to tear up our current agreement and have us sign a new one."

"Fine by me. Nice to see you again, Josiah, and thanks for the tip on this farm. Oh, by the way, I adopted three of those nags on Lady Elsmere's list and started paying for their upkeep. They'll retire to Wickliffe Farm."

I said "That's a kind gesture, Rudy. I'm sure Lady Elsmere was pleased."

"Doing what I can to fit in. I need to get back to work. See ya later."

"Or not," I replied.

Rudy gave me a quick smile, turned, and walked back to the barn.

Hunter said, "We were getting the stalls ready when you arrived. His horses are coming tomorrow."

"Don't worry. It was jolting seeing him here, that's all."

"I'm sure it was. I'm miffed Rudy didn't mention it himself."

"I didn't tell him that we were dating. I just said you were looking for a tenant."

"I'm sure Franklin would have mentioned us," Hunter said, running his thumb across his bottom lip.

"Let's not look a gift horse in the mouth."

"This hocus-pocus murder business has thrown me. I don't like the notion of it. Still, this check will keep me out of more debt."

"How are your loans coming along?"

Hunter put his arm around my waist and walked me to Wickliffe Manor. "I see the light at the end of the tunnel. I'm hoping to pay off everything by next year. Keeping my fingers crossed."

"I know you've been working very hard the past year."

"And you've been a doll about it. I'm afraid I'll be away for a lot of time this year again. This makes me worry about us."

"You do what you need to do, Hunter. I'm not going anywhere."

Hunter bent down and kissed me. "Once I get my personal finances in order, I want us to have a serious talk."

"About what?"

"Taking our relationship to the next level."

"How many ex-wives do you have?" I teased. "Two or is it three?"

"Oh, shut up. You know my ex-wives adore me. You talk to them often enough."

"I like them. You picked lovely women. I don't know why you divorced them."

"I didn't. They divorced me. Said I worked too much and was never home. Josiah, stay on track."

"Okay," I laughed. "We'll talk next year. I'm in no hurry. I like the way things are now."

"Nothing ever stays the same. We need to move forward."

"Right now, I need something to eat. How about fixing me a sandwich, boyfriend?"

"Coming right up, my lady." Hunter and I went inside discussing the repairs he still needed to make on the farm and the latest murder case he was working on, although he couldn't tell me much—not even the names involved. Just the barest details. Hunter was a forensic psychiatrist who profiled crime scenes.

Strange talk over a meal? Oh, I don't mind discussing murder as long as it is not my murder. That's where I draw the line.

6

I had decided to sell eggs at the farmers market as well as my honey. It required the least labor input for additional income. I was doing fine, finally making it into the black after five long years of money flying out of my hands. All my bills were paid on time, and I had extra money for luxuries like pedicures and professional haircuts. I even updated my wardrobe with new outfits and especially work boots—a must in my line of work. The Butterfly and the farm were free and clear, and my medical bills were up-to-date.

Renting out the Butterfly for wedding receptions and other events was proving to be a cash cow, so I decided to eliminate the tours. My partner, Eunice Todd, proved to be a maestro with handing all the details. I was in charge of the accounts and kept the Butterfly looking shipshape while Eunice handled the reception food, waiters, renting of dishware, tables, and chairs plus the setup and takedown, flowers, and any special requests. We guaranteed our clients that our food came from local farms directly to the table. What I didn't have in my private garden, Eunice bought from my farming buddies. If we couldn't find it locally, we didn't serve it. My walk-in freezer was stocked full of frozen vegetables, herbs, and fruits while bundles of flowers were drying in my barn to be used during the winter.

Barring an emergency, it seemed like this would be another good year. I was thinking I might even pull ahead and put some money into my savings. All I had to fall back on was my professor's pension from the University of Kentucky and a small CD. Most of my important works of art had been sold for repairs to the Butterfly. I still could sell the Butterfly, but I was determined not to because I was afraid a realtor would get a hold of the farm and turn this bit of heaven into a subdivision. Not on my watch.

So chickens were my new addiction. The income I got from their eggs was to pay for the animal feed needed in the winter, only my hens weren't laying. I called in water-witcher, Velvet Maddox, to help me discover the problem. I had first met Miss Velvet when she had rehabilitated Shaneika's racehorse, Comanche, from a lazy, ungrateful, angry hay-eating horse into a stakes winner. Turned out Velvet discovered Comanche had an infection near his eye socket. Once that was treated, Comanche started winning races, even coming in second at the Kentucky Derby. Lost by a nose, but we won't go into that now as it is still a sore subject with Shanieka Mary Todd, my criminal lawyer and friend.

Velvet pulled up in her huge pickup truck and jumped out. A shriveled, little pint of a woman, she looked out of place next to her expensive jacked-up ride. Velvet's hair had turned white since the last time I saw her and was tied in a long braid down her back. She wore a large, floppy straw hat with a wide brim plus a long sleeve cotton shirt and navy corduroy pants.

"Velvet, you're gonna need a stepladder to get back into your truck," I said, faintly amused.

"Ha ha, like I've never heard that one before. I like to sit up high so I can see everything."

"No, really. How are you going to get back in that monster?"

"You're going to give me a boost."

"Like hell I am."

Velvet grinned. "Nice to see you, too, Josiah."

Realizing Velvet was teasing, I relaxed. I was nothing but full of spit and vinegar due to stress, but then who wasn't. I took a deep breath. "I am much obliged you came, Velvet. I'm hoping you can help me."

"What seems to be the problem?"

"My hens aren't laying."

"How many ya got?"

"Twenty."

"What breeds?"

"Four each of Rhode Island Reds, White Leghorns, Ameraucanas, Marans, and Easter Eggers."

Velvet chuckled. "You're going to sell boutique eggs."

"Kind of. My goal is to have a United Nations of white, beige, chocolate brown, blue, and green eggs in one carton and sell them as organic eggs from free-range and non-caged chickens." The Rhode Island Reds lay beige eggs, White Leghorns lay white eggs, Ameraucanas and Easter Eggers lay various shades of blue and green eggs, while the Marans lay chocolate brown eggs. All of the eggs have deep yellow yolks. But my idea to have a cornucopia of egg colors in a reusable cardboard carton isn't taking off as planned.

"You know the eggs won't be a uniform size."

"Not selling them for their size. Selling them for their unique color and taste."

"I guess you're going to put a huge price on these eggs."

"Of course. Why be in business if not to make money?"

"Should be a hit with the city folk, Josiah. Now, let's go look at them chickens. Not laying you say?"

"I've tried everything. I must be doing something wrong."

"Not necessarily. Chickens are sensitive creatures. Anything can put them off."

Velvet followed me into my back yard where the

chickens were. "You let them out every day to forage?"

"Yes, ma'am. They usually stay in front of the house, or I put them in the garden. It is amazing how many insects they eat, but I don't let them near my hives."

"What about at night?"

"I put them back in their coop."

"Clean water?"

"Changed every day."

"What about cleanliness?"

"The coop is cleaned every week, and the waste is taken to the compost pile."

"I see you don't separate the different species."

"They seem to be getting along, but one White Leghorn bullies the others. I can't make her stop. See her? There she goes again chasing another chicken."

"She is the alpha hen and is keeping order as she sees it."

"Should I interfere with her? She pecks on the other hens."

"Josiah, I wouldn't. Not unless she's plucking out feathers or creating bare spots on the others. It's what the alpha hen does."

"I see."

"Going to get a rooster?"

"Absolutely not. They are too noisy, and I don't like the thought of selling fertilized eggs."

Velvet sighed. "You've told me enough. Go inside

while I talk with the hens and see what they've got to say to me. I expect a cold beer in a frosted mug waiting for me when I come in."

"How about a nice piece of blackberry cobbler as well?"

"I could do with some cobbler. Now, scoot, Josiah. I've got work to do."

I went inside as ordered and heated up a bowl of blackberry cobbler and poured a mug of a craft beer made just a few miles from me. I don't like beer as a rule, but I keep a supply because many of my friends enjoy it. Since the entire back of my house is glass, I could watch Velvet commune with my chickens. Several chickens came to Velvet, and it looked like they were holding an actual conversation with her. They'd cackle, and she would respond. I didn't doubt for one moment that they were speaking with one another.

Velvet was known for her intimacy with creatures and nine times of out ten, her advice was right on the money. She was a darling of the Thoroughbred crowd and a go-to person for me when my critters needed help and my vet threw up his hands, not knowing what to do.

After a few moments of conversing with my hens, Velvet came inside the Butterfly and sat at my Nakashima dining room table. I placed a heaping bowl of warm blackberry cobbler with a scoop of vanilla ice cream and a chilled mug of beer before her.

ABIGAIL KEAM

I had the same, but with a mug of hot tea. "What's up with my girls?"

Velvet took a sip of beer, leaving a foamy mustache on her upper lip. She licked it off. "You've got a fox problem. This fox comes every night looking for a way into the coop. He's making your chickens mighty nervous. So nervous they aren't relaxed enough to lay eggs."

"Hmm."

"Have you noticed any digging around the coop?"

"Yes, but I thought it was Baby," I said, referring to my English Mastiff who was napping in his bed by the couch.

"If your dog was near the coop, he's probably smelling the fox."

"What should I do?"

"Most people would kill the fox."

"I hate to kill an animal who is trying to survive. Any other suggestions?"

"You can urinate around the coop."

"Excuse me?"

"Get some man to pee around the coop. Urine is how animals mark their territory. Might scare the fox off."

"It will scare me off."

"The fox is not going to leave your chickens alone."

"What about an electric fence around the coop?"

"Possibly might do the trick. Also crushed garlic

46

and chili peppers around the coop will help. They don't like their odor." Velvet took a bite of the blackberry cobbler, pushing aside the vanilla ice cream. "You can also leave chocolate, raisins, and grapes out. Those will hurt a fox as well. Might not kill the fox, but will slow it down."

"You call yourself a healer? Geez, Velvet." I sighed. What to do? What to do?

"Get rid of the fox and your hens will lay."

"Thank you for the advice. I'll think of something to do with the fox." I took a spoonful of my cobbler.

Velvet said, "I want to talk about something else."

"Okay."

"I understand you crossed swords with gloom and doom Lettie Lemore."

"You know her?"

"We're competitors in the horse whispering trade. She's stealing my clients."

"What do you think of her?"

"Right now she's the darling of the big horse owners. A shiny new toy. I think she's got talent, but she's not very discreet nor does she practice common sense."

"And you do?" I teased.

Velvet huffed, "I certainly wouldn't tell someone they were going to commit murder. Some people are very susceptible to suggestion. Just saying such a thing might put that idea in someone's head."

"Do you think she's legit?"

"I've never met her and haven't heard anything scandalous, but she came out of nowhere. Never heard of her before a year ago."

"Is she a Kentuckian?"

"Don't know. She doesn't talk about her past. She's got a website, but scant information about her. Just lots of boot-licking testimonies from grateful clients."

"I talked with her at Lady Elsmere's party, and she has a Midwestern accent. She could be from anywhere."

"Like I said, she's a mystery."

"What exactly did you hear about murder and from whom?"

"I heard the story from Shaneika Todd."

"Shaneika? I haven't spoken to her for weeks."

"Comanche is studding at Darby Dan farm. I ran into Shaneika in the breeding shed."

"She wasn't even at the fundraiser where I encountered Lettie, so I'm wondering how she knew."

"Apparently from your friend, Franklin."

I nodded. "Makes sense. Do you know the entire story?"

"From what I understand, a Rudy Lee is to murder you and then be murdered by someone else."

"That's the crux of it."

"Like I said it was an irresponsible fortune to tell. I would never say such a thing, even if I thought it to be true."

"You would not warn someone if you thought they were going to be harmed?"

Velvet thought for a moment. "It would have to be a very strong sensation for me to do so. That's a lot of negative energy to throw someone's way."

"That's what Lemore said of me. She said I had negative energy emanating from me."

Velvet gave me a steady look. "Your aura is fine, Josiah. There's nothing evil about you. Maybe too much curiosity and stubbornness for your own good, but that's all. Remember curiosity killed the cat."

"Gee, thanks," I said.

"Did you tell Franklin about the fortune?"

"Franklin drove Rudy Lee home. Rudy must have told him the story in the car."

Velvet wiped her nose with a clean bandanna. "Sounds like a hoax."

"Really? That's good to hear."

"Do you know the man well?"

"Never met him before Lady Elsmere's party. She was the entertainment at the party. Rudy was pretty shook up after he spoke with Lemore. I saw him again at Hunter Wickliffe's farm. He is leasing it for his Standardbred horses."

Velvet asked, "How did he seem to you then?"

"Like it didn't bother him anymore. I think he put Lettie Lemore's fortune behind him."

"How did you react to seeing him again?"

"It threw me off, I must admit. I may not believe in Lemore's prediction, but why tempt fate? I'm going to stay away from Wickliffe Manor. If Hunter wants to see me, he can come here."

"I'd forget about Lemore, Josiah." Velvet's words were reassuring, so why did she look concerned?

"Do you sense anything, Velvet? Is danger coming my way? What do you see?"

Velvet closed her eyes and waved her hands in a circle, mumbling, "I see the future, Josiah. The mists are parting. The path is becoming clearer and clearer to me. I see you. Yes, I see you calling to me. You are reaching out to me."

"Am I saying anything?"

"You are handing me something. Something very precious."

"What is it?"

Velvet slammed her hands on the table. "I have it! You are going to get me another bowl of blackberry cobbler."

"You old coot!" Laughing, I snatched her bowl and got Velvet another helping of blackberry cobbler without ice cream this time. I may have been laughing on the outside, but I was concerned. One thing I have noticed about people, especially women is that they are too trusting. They think something horrible is never going to happen to them and don't recognize danger when it's coming their way.

I'm the opposite. I see danger around every corner. I jump if a car horn blares, a baby cries, or a donkey brays. There are mysterious forces which invade our lives, and evil people walk beside us. I'm very much like the cavewoman hunkered down by her fire in a cave on a stormy night, fearing the outside and the unknown. Yep, I'm a coward at heart.

So, when a seer says someone is going to murder me, I take it seriously, even though I know intellectually it makes no sense. What made it worse was I knew Velvet was lying to me about the seriousness of the situation and was taking Lettie Lemore's foretelling to heart.

Jumping Jehoshaphat!

7

"Do you have to watch?" Matt asked, unzipping his pants.

"You don't have anything I haven't seen before," I replied, amused at Matt's sudden modesty.

Matt was my best friend who lived in a bungalow on my property. He looked like the 40s actor, Victor Mature—you know, tall, dark, and swarthy. Mature was also funny as evident in this quote, "Hollywood is a place where the stars twinkle until they wrinkle."

"You're looking at me like a hungry toad spotting a fly."

"Very well," I turned my back on Matt and the coop, feeding the chickens some corn. "Make sure you pee all around the coop."

"How often am I supposed to do this?"

"As many times as you can for a couple of days until I get an electric fence up." I broadcast the mixed corn. "Here, chick, chick. Here, chick, chick."

Matt muttered, "The things I do for you."

"You are sweet to do this. I promise I will go to the feed store today and see if they have some sort of predator repellant, but for now you're the repellant."

"When is the fence going up?" Matt asked, zipping up his pants.

"Can I turn around now?"

"I'm decent."

"The fence will go up as soon as you can spare the time to help me put it up."

"Oh, goodie. Another time suck."

"It shouldn't take more than a couple of hours. After all, you do live rent free in my cabana."

"On which I do all the maintenance for free. You didn't pay a dime for repairing that shack, and you don't pay a dime on its upkeep now."

"I paid for all the upgrades, landscaping, and what-nots, plus still pay for its mowing and taxes if you remember. I grant that you put in the elbow grease."

Matt burst out laughing. "Oh, Josiah, you are so easy."

"I fall for that same gag every time, don't I?" I replied, feeling the heat rising to my cheeks.

"Of course, I'll help you put up the fence. Get the wiring and I'll put it up tomorrow." Matt came over and grabbed my shoulder, giving me a big squeeze. "What's the matter, honey pie? You seem all tense."

"I am. I know it's stupid because of the reason why."

"Is it that fortune teller spouting you were going to be murdered?"

My eyes widened. "You know?"

"Yep. Franklin can't keep a secret."

"I should have known. How long?"

"Franklin called me the night he took Rudy Lee home. He said Mr. Lee was really shook up and taking the fortune seriously."

"Lee changed his mind because he leased Hunter's farm."

Matt's brow knitted. "You know this Lee?"

"Never met him before. The family was in sugar. June had business dealings with his father. That's how she knows him."

"What would June have to do with sugar?"

"I dunno."

"Do you have any connection with Lee other than meeting him at the party?"

"Besides having Hunter in common now—no."

"My advice is to stay away from Hunter's farm and cross the street if you see Lee downtown."

"So you think there is an inkling of truth to this story?"

"I think all things are interconnected. Why take a chance, Jo?"

I raised my eyebrows in dismay. "I've never known you to be superstitious."

"Before I met you, I would have considered this all

bunk. But so much has happened to the both of us, I take a more cautious approach to life."

I felt a twinge of guilt since Matt had been shot by a rogue cop trying to kill me at Cumberland Falls. I don't think he ever recovered physically or emotionally from it, but we never discuss it. "What does Franklin think? I haven't seen him for a while."

"He thinks it's a big hoax to garner Lemore some free publicity."

"I don't see how that would work in Lemore's favor unless I was actually murdered."

"Precisely."

I drew back. "Oh! You think Lemore and Lee are working together on some type of scam?"

Matt waved a fly away. "How is he paying Hunter's lease?"

"He paid via check. It was in the high five figures for six months."

"I would be interested to see if the check went through. Do you know?"

I shook my head. "Hunter had to go out of town on business. I usually don't talk to him unless he calls me since he's usually on a crime scene or in court."

"I see. Well, I think that is high even for Hunter's farm. I would have asked for a cashier's check."

"Lee leased the entire four hundred acres and all of the barns."

"My advice is to hide the silver until the check is

secured in Hunter's bank account. And Josiah?"

"Yeah?"

"For once, use your head. Stay away from Wickliffe Manor and soothsayers for the time being. Something could be afoot."

"Okay, Sherlock." But the look on Matt's face was seriously disturbing. Did he know something I didn't? Or were we both being chicken?

8

Matt and I put up the electric fence the next day. Franklin sat on a blanket with Emmeline, Matt's baby, while we worked. Once in a while, a chicken would come over and cackle at the baby to which she would clasp her hands in delight and gurgle a laugh. Naturally, Franklin was frightened of the birds and would shoo them away.

"They're not going to hurt you," I said.

Franklin retorted, "I don't like how they give me the eye from their tiny little heads."

"They are curious and think you might have something to eat. Crumble up some of the baby's crackers and throw out to them. Make friends."

"I'd rather eat them for dinner."

"The crackers or the hens?"

"Both. How long do you think it takes to pluck the feathers off a chicken?"

"Shush now. We've had enough talk about death around here. Besides, I'm trying to get them to lay eggs."

"I don't see how you're going to make any money on eggs. By the time you take out the cost of the coop, feed, and now the fence, it will take years to recoup your investment." Franklin used his finger in the air to do mathematical equations. "Twenty chickens laying an egg each for six days is one hundred and twenty eggs. Then divide that by twelve and then you have only ten cartons of eggs. How are you going to make money on ten cartons of eggs a week?"

"This is only the first stage. If I am successful, then I will purchase more hens. I didn't want to get in over my head at first."

Franklin asked, "What are you going to do with the hens when they stop laying eggs?"

I scratched my head. "Haven't gotten that far yet."

"Look around. This is nothing but an animal sanctuary. Sheep, llamas, cats, old horses, goats, peacocks, and everything in between. All they do is eat and poop."

"They add ambience."

"They cost a fortune to maintain. You're not rich like Lady Elsmere to underwrite an animal sanctuary."

Matt pounded in the last stake. "Franklin, give Josiah a break. You've been on a rant about these chickens ever since she got them. Let's talk about something else."

"Yeah, let's," I agreed as I wrapped wire around the stakes.

Matt came behind me and secured the electrical wire.

I went over and sat with Franklin while Matt put on the finishing touches.

"Let's test this baby," he said, flipping a switch. "Franklin, come over here and touch the wires."

Franklin made a face. "Ha ha. Very funny."

Matt gingerly touched the top wire with his index finger. "Ouch." He pulled back. "She's working." He flipped off the switch. "Just flip this button on when you put the ladies to bed, and I think that should take care of your fox problem."

I said, "Thanks, guys. I appreciate your help."

Matt came over and joined us on the blanket.

Emmeline held up her arms. Matt picked his baby up and put her in his lap. "Franklin, can you hand me her bottle?" Watching the two interact, Matt caught me. "What are you grinning at?"

"Just thinking of how you used to be—a sex machine about town. Now look at you."

Matt clasped his hands over Emmeline's ears. "The baby doesn't have to know about my sordid past. I thank you not to mention it."

Franklin quipped, "You mean your glory days as sex on a stick?"

"Shut up both of you."

I said, "You look happy, Matt."

He put his chin on top of his baby's head. "I am

content. On a beautiful day like today and with the most important people in my life at my side, how can I not be happy?"

Franklin started to say something.

"Be quiet, Franklin. Don't spoil this moment," Matt said.

Franklin shrugged and lay back on the blanket. Matt fed Emmeline as I leaned against an old oak tree, listening to honeybees buzzing about us and the occasional cry of my peacocks. It couldn't get any better than this.

But our peace wouldn't last. We should have known.

9

I was in my Prius heading over to Hunter's house. I knew I said I was going to stay away, but Hunter was out of town and Franklin wanted me to check on the house. Rudy had called Franklin to say lights were flashing inside the house.

In hindsight, I don't know why I didn't have Franklin call the police. Franklin couldn't leave work, and he thought it was just a fuse that had gone bad. "Be a dear and check for me. I can't get there until I finish this assignment, and I don't want the house to burn down on my watch." Since he had babysat Emmeline so Matt could help with the electric fence, I obliged, especially after he said Rudy was heading home. I believed Rudy and I would not set eyes upon each other, so Baby and I drove toward Wickliffe Manor.

It was a gorgeous day, and I could smell the earth coming to life again after a hard winter. I felt joyous and Baby was in a good mood, too. I sang along with the radio as Baby occasionally howled in concert with me. Finally, nearing the entrance to the Wickliffe Manor, I flipped on my left turn signal and slowed down, waiting for a car in the other lane to pass before I turned into the winding driveway of the farm. The two magnificent metal gates that provided security were open. I was concerned as Hunter always kept them closed when he was away.

I stopped the car once past them and punched in the code at the keypad station inside the gates. They moved a bit, making weird metallic scraping noise and then came to a screeching halt.

Since the gates were almost a hundred years old, I got out of the car to inspect the problem. "Stay here, Baby." I went over to the gates and punched in the codes again at the keypad station at the road entrance, knowing I could rush inside while the gates were moving. The gates still did not respond.

I tugged on the gates, which would not budge. They were too heavy for me to coax. Figuring this was an electrical problem with the keypad, I decided to check on the house and then call Franklin. He would have to deal with the gates as this was above my pay grade. I was opening my car door when I heard a cracking sound. My small pea brain must have recognized the sound because I ran like the dickens. A loud pop, crash, and then silence. I turned and froze. A huge limb had fallen on my car, smashing in the hood. I screamed, "BABY! BABY!" and ran to my Prius feverishly trying to pull a car door open, but I couldn't budge the limb. The roof was so caved in I couldn't even see into the front of the car. "BABY!"

I ran into the road flagging down any car as my phone was in the car. Now when I say ran, I mean more like a hobbled trot, but I went as fast as I could. A red pickup truck stopped, and a man, wearing a John Deere hat and khaki work clothes, leaned out of his window looking weary. "What's the matter, lady?"

"Oh please, a big limb fell on my car and I don't hear my dog! Can you help me? Look in the driveway, you can see it. I must know if my dog is all right."

The man glanced over and seeing the situation, pulled his truck into the driveway. He jumped down and bent the seat back, pulling out a small chainsaw.

When I saw the chainsaw, I almost wept and followed the man to my car.

"Have mercy, that's quite a mess," he said, pushing back his cap and perusing my car hood crushed in with the giant limb splayed across the top of my Prius.

I tugged at the limb. "Hurry. Hurry. My dog might be injured."

He revved up his chainsaw and began cutting the limb as I removed away the cut sections. Finally, I pulled away a section where Baby had been sitting. He wasn't in the seat. Where was he? I tried to pull the door open, but it was stuck.

To my relief, I heard a whimper and then a low

growl. "Baby." I pressed my hands and face against the passenger's front window and saw movement in the back. "Here. Here. Cut here," I begged the man. Within minutes, I was tugging on the back door where I could see Baby looking back at me. He looked stunned and frightened, but wagged his tail when he saw me. "I'm coming, Baby. We'll get you out." I turned to the man. "Can you help me please?"

The man tugged on the back door, but couldn't get it open. "Wait here," he said, going to his truck. Coming back with a hammer and a face shield, he told me to call Baby to the other side of the car. "Need to get this big boy out of the way."

I hurried to the other side of the car. "Baby. Baby, come to me."

As Baby leapt to the other side of the car, the man broke the window and reached in unlocking the door and pulling it open. Seeing freedom, Baby sprang out of the car, barking furiously. I rushed over to him. "Baby, calm down. Calm down."

"That's a big dog, lady. Will he bite me?"

"No. No. He's gentle. He must have jumped into the back seat to watch me when I fiddled with the gate. Oh, he is a lucky, lucky dog," I said, inspecting Baby.

Disoriented and shaking, Baby managed to sniff me and give a kiss with his tongue. "You're okay. Shake it off, Baby. We are both fine."

"Is he okay, ma'am?"

Seeing no blood and or injuries, I rose to thank the Samaritan. "Sir, I can't thank you enough. I don't know what I would have done if you hadn't stopped for me."

"I think you should call the police."

Getting my phone out of the car, I said, "I'm calling my insurance company right now."

"I think you need to call the police first."

"Why?"

"Look here, ma'am." He pointed to the junction of the limb, where it had separated from the oak tree. Half of it had been sawed through. "This is negligence for sure. Someone started to cut this limb and then walked away before the job was completed. It's a fresh cut, too. I say this was done today. Do you live here? Your maintenance crew sure is irresponsible."

"I don't live here."

The man looked at me inquisitively.

"I was to check on the house and stopped to check the gates. They're not supposed to be open."

"I'd call the owner and give him a what for. This limb could have killed you. Good thing you were out of the car." The man looked at the Prius and whistled. "I hope you have good insurance. I think this car may be totaled. It's a shame. Looked like a nice car, but then you 'n your dog are alive. That's the important thing."

The blood in my veins chilled, but I said nothing.

After getting the Samaritan's contact information, I saw him on his way. Then, Baby and I slowly walked to

Wickliffe Manor. Baby seemed to have recovered from his fright and lumbered toward the house ahead of me, but I jumped at every bird call and every snort from horses now grazing in the fields.

I sat on the steps of the mansion's massive portico. My hands were shaking so badly, I could barely dial 911. "Hello. Hello. My name is Josiah Reynolds, and I think someone just tried to kill me."

10

Franklin, Baby, and I watched the police take pictures of the oak tree where the limb had broken off and various pictures of the car. One of the officers walked over to us and petted Baby. His name tag read—RILEY. "Whose car is this?"

"Mine," I answered.

"Are you the one who called 911?"

"Yes."

"You said something about someone trying to kill you?"

"I'm sure you have seen the limb was sawed halfway through from the trunk of the tree."

"We saw that, but it's an odd way to kill someone." He wiped his brow with a handkerchief. "How would the murderer know your car would stop under the limb, and what caused it to fall at that particular moment?"

"That would be the most likely place for me to park the car when checking on the gates. As you see, the oak tree stands next to the driveway, and the limb hung over the road. It was so pretty. It framed the driveway so. A shame someone cut it."

"Why were you checking on the gates?"

"They were open for one thing. Mr. Wickliffe likes to have them closed for security reasons."

Officer Riley looked at Franklin. "Are you who she's talking about?"

"Mrs. Reynolds is referring to my brother who lives here. This is a family estate."

"Where's your brother and what's his name?" Riley asked, poising his pen in midair.

"My brother is Hunter Wickliffe, and he is in Las Vegas working on a case?"

Riley glanced up from his notes. "A case? Is he a cop?"

"He is a forensic psychiatrist who helps the police on crime scenes."

"Hmm," Riley muttered, writing this information down. He looked back at me. "Then what happened?"

"I drove through the gates and stopped the car to punch in the keypad. You can see the keypad station is next to the oak tree. When the gates didn't close, I got out of the car to check both keypads but to no avail. I then tried to close the gates myself, but they were too heavy for me."

"Uh huh," Officer Riley said, writing.

Franklin and I exchanged glances.

"I called Mrs. Reynolds to come and check the house for me," Franklin said.

"Why?"

"The tenant said lights were flashing inside the house. I couldn't get off work, so I asked Mrs. Reynolds to check the house for me."

"Why didn't you ask the tenant to check for you?"

"He doesn't have a key to the house. Mrs. Reynolds does."

Looking at my driver's license, the officer said, "I see you live near the Kentucky River near Lexington. That's a long drive from here."

I replied, "It takes me about thirty-five minutes."

Officer Riley said, "I still don't know why you think someone is trying to kill you, Mrs. Reynolds. Anybody could have come through the gate and had the same experience as you."

"I think I was set up." I remember Hunter telling me that even an accusation of murder without proof could tie me up in court for years on a slander charge from the accused. I merely replied, "I don't know. The whole thing seems fishy."

Officer Riley said, "It looks like an unfortunate accident to me."

I merely said, "You're right. I am overreacting."

Franklin shot me a curious look, but decided to play along. "Officer, why don't you talk with the tenant? Perhaps he saw someone on the property, but Mrs.

Reynolds is correct. Something is fishy. I checked the keypad stations, and a wire had been pulled loose."

"Maybe it just came loose."

"No, sir. The copper wire had been stretched. Someone pulled it."

"What did you say your tenant's name was?"

"Rutherford Robert Lee."

I asked, "Can you just talk to Lee please? I would like to have his replies on official record."

"Are you implying Mr. Lee tried to kill you, ma'am?"

"I'm not saying anything of the sort. Just talk to him. Okay?"

Franklin gave Officer Riley Rudy's contact information, as we watched the police pack up and leave.

We glumly walked to Wickliffe Manor where Franklin checked the lights and the fuse box. Everything worked perfectly and the fuses were fine.

Franklin and I gravitated toward the kitchen where he pulled two sodas from the fridge. I pulled the tab on mine. "Lordy, what a day."

"Josiah, I am so sorry. I'm quite at a loss of what to say. Your poor car."

"I'll have it towed this week. I'm too bushed to deal with it today." I peered out the open door. "It's getting late. I have to get home."

"Stay here for the night."

"I can't. I have to get back to put my chickens up in

the coop and turn on the fence."

"Ah, the quick red fox."

"Take me to the nearest car rental business. I'm sure they are still open."

"Let me lock up the house first. Wait for me under the portico."

"Make it fast, Franklin."

I sat in a rocker behind a massive white column and waited. While I waited, I felt anger—the type of anger I hadn't felt for a long time. It wasn't a pleasant sensation and it seemed directed at everyone—Lettie Lemore for her creepy prediction, Hunter for not being home, Franklin for asking me to come, Rudy for putting this accident in motion, and most of all, myself for being so stupid as to fall for one of the oldest tricks in the book. I was sure Rudy had fabricated the flashing light story to get me out here.

Haven't I always said women never see the danger coming their way, even when it's right in front of them?

I felt like a fool.

11

I got home just in time to hear a lot of squawking. The fox was after my chickens! Baby and I ran into the back yard, and upon seeing the fox, Baby ran her off, but we were too late. The fox had gotten one of my White Leghorns. What a rotten day this had been. I put the chickens up for the night and turned on the electric fence.

Maybe keeping chickens was not a good idea. The Butterfly was on the cusp of the Palisades where many predators lived.

Picking up the dead chicken by the legs, I said a prayer. "So sorry, little girl, but I tried to get home as fast as I could." I felt terrible about this. Even chickens feel dread when they are about to be devoured. What to do with her? There was no need to waste the chicken. She was killed for food, so I threw her carcass into the woods, knowing the fox would find her.

How could I be angry with the fox? She was trying to survive with the skills and instinct nature had given her.

Weren't we all?

There is only one thing to do when one has had a terrible day—go to bed. I took a shower, put out some clean clothes for tomorrow, did a load of laundry, and finally plopped onto my bed.

Baby came over and put his rough paw on my arm. He whined a little and his eyes looked sympathetic.

"Oh, Baby, you're such a good friend." I patted his paw. "You go to bed now. Everything is okay. Things will look brighter in the morning."

A cat jumped on the bed.

"Or maybe not."

Another cat jumped on my bed. Then another. The Kitty Kaboodle gang had finished eating in the kitchen and were now joining Baby and me for slumber time. Another one was on my vanity knocking my makeup to the floor. The cats were Baby's pets, but I was the one who housed, medicated, and fed them. Baby just played with them. I pushed the cats off my bed, but no matter. They joined Baby in his bed—all five of them, plus the mother of the brood.

I exhaled. Maybe Franklin was right. I wasn't running a farm, but a zoo. But the problem was the animals were running me.

Jumping Jehoshaphat! This was getting out of hand!

12

After spending an hour on the phone with Hunter's insurance company, I received the news the repairs would cost more than the worth of the Prius, so they totaled it. However, the check for the car would not provide for a new one. I would either have to go into debt again to purchase a new car or get a used car. I have no problem driving a used car, but the check wouldn't cover what I wanted in a used car either. I needed something large enough to store my products for the farmers market. Since market day was coming up, I needed to do something fast, so I went hat in hand to see Charles, June's heir.

I found Charles in his office amidst contracts, personnel schedules, and lots of notes stuck to the wall behind him. "Josiah, this is a surprise."

"Sorry to bother you, Charles, but I need a favor."

"How may I help you?"

"I need to borrow a small truck with a cap for some time. Do you have one available?"

"I've got one, but it's kind of beat up."

"Does it run?"

"Purrs like a kitten."

"That's fine then. I just need transportation." I told Charles what had happened to my Prius, but left out that I thought it has been a plot to murder me.

"The insurance company should provide a rental car for you."

"They are, but as soon as the check for the Prius is issued, they will revoke the rental."

"Well, that is some strange story you're telling me."

"Let me switch subjects while I'm here. You were at the party. Did you see anything unusual?"

"As far as I knew, everyone had a good time. June raised some money, and all the horses got a good home. By the way, you need to pick your horse up. He's in the back paddock."

"He? I thought I was getting a mare."

"Nope. It's a he, all right."

I made a face. Stallions are always more difficult to care for than mares. Especially hot bloods. I usually had to put them in a double-fenced paddock to keep them away from the other horses. "I must have ticked the wrong name. Give me a couple of days first."

The phone rang and Charles answered it. He was busy and I was taking up his time. I rose, but Charles motioned me to sit. Apparently, one of the horses had swallowed a plastic bag that had blown into her field,

ABIGAIL KEAM

which is why I'm always railing against littering. People throw garbage out of their cars not thinking that someone or something else is going to have to pay for their thoughtlessness. The wind carries the debris into the fields and no matter how many times the fields are checked, some of the litter can be ingested by an animal. Now a pregnant mare was in distress, and a vet had to be called.

Shaking his head, Charles got off the phone. "That field was inspected this morning before we let the horses out to pasture. Makes me so mad."

"Is she down?"

"She's standing, but showing signs of weakening. The boys have brought her back to the barn."

"I hope the vet can do something."

Charles nodded. "You were asking me about the party."

"Yes."

"Sorry, Josiah, but I didn't notice anything out of kilter."

"Did you talk to Rudy Lee?"

"Just for a few minutes."

"May I ask what about?"

"Apparently you had spoken to him about leasing Wickliffe Manor. He asked if I could vouch for Hunter's character and if I thought it was a suitable farm."

"Anything else?"

76

"He asked about you."

"In what way?"

"He seemed to know you were dating Hunter and asked if the relationship was serious."

"That's odd. I never told him that I was dating Hunter."

"I told him I didn't know."

"June said she had business dealings with his father. Did you know him?"

"Way before my time."

"What about Lettie Lemore?"

Charles made a face. He was a religious man and didn't hold cotton to soothsayers in any form. "As far as I know she came, told people what they wanted to hear, got paid, and left."

"No complaints?"

"None that I know of. Should there have been?"

"Just wondering. I understand horse owners consider Lemore a horse whisperer. June ever use her?"

"Not on my watch. I don't even like June engaging Velvet Maddox, but she's still the boss, so if June wants Velvet, she gets Velvet."

The phone rang again. Charles answered it and said, "Hold please." He picked up a key ring set from the key safe on the wall and tossed it to me. "Truck is in the equipment barn. Tell the boys I said you could use it. No rush bringing it back. We're not using it."

"Thanks, Charles."

I rose and quietly shut the office door. I kissed the keys, thinking my luck was changing.

Boy, was I wrong!

13

I loaded the truck with my honey, table, chair, umbrella, and cashbox with a hundred dollars in change. Since I had the rest of the day free, I spent it searching the internet for any information about Lettie Lemore and Rutherford Robert Lee. I found several newspaper articles on Rudy Lee or rather his father and his business ventures, but the most recent article was twenty years old, and the old man was long since dead. Nothing about Rudy Lee himself.

I could find nothing on Lettie Lemore until she put up shop in Louisville and became the new darling of the horsey set. I concluded Lettie Lemore was a professional name and not her legal one. Hmm. I needed to find out her real name, so I put in a call on my rotary phone to Matt. "Hey, Matt. I need a favor. It's very important that you help with this."

"Whatcha need, red-headed goddess?"

"I need you to turn on that sex-machine thingy you've got and go see a lady."

There was silence on Matt's end of the phone for a few seconds. "Excuse me?"

"I need pre-Meriah Matt and not post baby-daddy Matt to turn on the charm—or have you lost your mojo?"

I could actually hear Matt grin. Yes—grin.

"Who will be the poor victim of my wit and charisma?"

"A fortune teller named Lettie Lemore. Will you do it?"

"Anything for my queen."

I pulled the phone from my ear and stared at the mouthpiece before speaking again. "This was too easy. You must want something."

"Now that you mention it, my pitiable abode needs a new air conditioner."

"Okay, but if I buy a new air conditioner, will you pay rent?"

"You know, my chest still hurts where I took a bullet for you at Cumberland Falls, but I'll see what I can do."

I laughed. "You are the devil, Matt. You've got me over a barrel since I need your particular expertise. You've won. I'm texting you the number and address now. Make an appointment." I fumbled with my cell phone which was almost eight years old. I used my cell phone for texting and my rotary phone for speaking directly to a person. I did not see the need to combine the two.

"I'm looking at my mobile phone now. Your text is coming through. Lettie Lemore—the prophetess of doom? I heard all about the car incident from Franklin. I would consider it an honor to put the finger on her."

"And yet you never called to see how I was."

"I saw you drive by my house. You looked fine. Besides, from the expression on your face, you were planning something. I was biding my time until your phone call. See, Miss Lemore is not the only one with ESP."

"Just call and make an appointment. Give her a fake name. I'm sure lots of people do that. Tell her that you'll pay in cash when you come. Don't give her a credit card number."

"What's my undercover name?"

"Make something up. You're a lawyer. Lying should be second nature to you."

"Keep besmirching my profession, and you'll have to find yourself another boy."

"Just telephone the pigeon."

"Call you when I make contact."

"Roger." I hung up.

I drummed my fingers on my desk, dreaming up the next steps of my plan while considering the axiom, 'Revenge is a dish best served cold.'

I hoped I wasn't coming in too hot.

14

I waited in the car doing crossword puzzles while Matt went inside the office building for his appointment with Lemore. Yep, that's right. A clean, modern, efficient, and boring office building near a strip mall. I had been hoping the appointment would be in her home that was something unkempt, gloomy, and shimmering with dreary atmosphere.

Forty-five minutes later, Matt came back to his car. He got in and took off his wedding ring and glasses.

"Well?" I asked.

Leaning back against the car seat, Matt took some deep breaths. He seemed rattled. "She knew I was a fake."

"What do you mean?"

"She asked why I was wearing a wedding ring when I wasn't married and had never been married."

"What else did Lemore say?"

"She said I was not at peace because I had divided loyalties."

"What does that mean?"

"She said it was between a man and a woman, but I needed to make a choice."

"Oh. Meriah and Franklin."

"She didn't say so specifically, but that's how I interpreted it."

"What else?"

"She said I was surrounded by violence and darkness due to my association with one person, and I had already been terribly injured because of that association." Matt gave me a discerning look.

"You sure she didn't know who you are?"

"She said I was going to make important changes soon concerning my life."

"Such as?"

"She didn't know, but said they would be life altering because of my child."

"Did you tell her about Emmeline?"

Matt shook his head. "No, Jo. I didn't."

"It sounds like a threat to me."

"Or a warning."

"You think she's the real thing, don't you?"

"I do. I think she's legit. You better take her warning seriously."

"Oh, Matt, I'm so disappointed."

"I must admit she threw me, but don't despair. I think I got her real name."

"Oh, goody. How?"

"She went out of the room for coffee. I took the opportunity to peruse the mail on her desk. There was a letter addressed to a Zasu Pitts."

"Zasu Pitts! Now I know why she changed her name. I'd change it, too."

"Duck down! She's coming out of the building."

I slumped in my seat with my heart beating fast. Please don't walk near Matt's car. "Does she see you?"

"No, she's going to the other side of the parking lot. She's getting into a Mercedes."

"Business must be good."

"Stay down."

"Follow her, Matt!"

Matt turned on the ignition and followed at a discreet distance. "Jo, write down her license plate number."

"How can I cramped like this?"

"I'll read the numbers to you. Get something out of your purse to write on."

I fumbled around my purse and found a pen and a grocery receipt. "Ready."

Matt dictated the plate numbers, and I read them back to him.

"Perfect."

"Can I sit up now?"

"NO! Stay where you are."

"This is really uncomfortable, Matt. My neck is getting a crick." I felt the car turn. "Where are we heading?"

"Toward Cherokee Park."

"Fancy." An older and pricey neighborhood surrounded Cherokee Park, which was designed by Frederick Law Olmsted, who designed Central Park in New York City as well.

"What's happening?"

Matt said, "She's looking for a place to park."

"Where are we?"

"Facing the park."

"Does she notice you?"

"I don't think so." Matt parked his car further up the street. "You can sit up now. She wouldn't be able to see you at this angle."

"Thank goodness." I rubbed my neck looking around at the stunning Victorian houses. "Nice neighborhood. Isn't this the street where Sue Grafton, the mystery writer, lived?"

"I have no idea. I don't read mysteries."

"I do. I love them."

"Figures." Matt started the car. "I'm going to drive around the block and come back to get the house number." He drove around the block and came back to the street. "It's the house with the blue shutters and gingerbread on the porch."

I took a picture of the house with Matt's phone and wrote down its number. I now had something to work with.

Matt seemed concerned. "You'd think if she was

really psychic, she would have sensed us."

"Did she touch you?"

"No."

"She didn't ask to touch your hand or touch something that belonged to you?"

Matt shook his head as he drove back to Lexington. "Why?"

"Lemore told me that she received images from touch—psychometry. The problem with psychometry is that one can read the past or present, but not the future."

"Maybe she can do both."

"Maybe she's a fake."

"How did she know all about me then?"

"It's easy enough. You live on my farm and your story about being shot was in the newspaper. Also, she could have called Meriah Caldwell. It's easy to get information on you. All Lemore has to do is search on her computer."

"Hmm." Matt suddenly thought of something. "I wasn't at the party. How would she know what I looked like?"

"Again, the paper had photos of you, and your law firm has a picture of you on their website."

"Darn."

"Sorry, old boy."

"She said I was getting married within two years, and the marriage would be a happy one."

"Aren't you happy?"

"The baby has filled a huge void in my life. I feel content."

"I hear a 'but.'"

"I get lonely, Jo. My life is very full, but I still get lonely."

I didn't reply because I knew what he was saying. I also didn't tell him Lemore had predicted marriage for Franklin as well. Why stir a wasp nest up? So I spent the ride home planning my next step. But fate beat me to it. When I think I have control, it is ripped right out of my hands, but at least, I was alive.

That was more than I could say about Rutherford Robert Lee.

15

Hunter flew back after his insurance company contacted him about the car incident. He was understandably upset about the accident, but more for the fact that neither Franklin nor I had notified him of the event. Saying he was angry is putting it mildly.

Pacing in my living room like a caged tiger, Hunter berated me for my lack of judgment. He went on for several minutes about this and that until I said in a very loud and clear voice, "SHUT UP!"

Stunned that I dared to contradict him while ranting, Hunter asked, "What did you say?"

"I said shut up. You are not my father, and I am not fourteen. You have no right to speak to me so. I went over to Wickliffe Manor to help you out, and all I got for my trouble is a wrecked car, so shut up."

"But."

"There are no buts. Stop pacing. Stop yelling. I won't have it. If you can't control yourself, get out."

"I'm so angry."

"I know you're angry and I don't care. I lost interest in men's anger a long time ago, nor will I be bothered to fix men's anger. That's why I didn't call you. You lash out when you're frightened."

Hunter plopped down beside me on the couch. "I am scared, Jo, but you should have warned me. When I got the call about the insurance, I was floored. Then I got home and inspected the tree. The police were right. Someone cut that limb! You could have been seriously hurt or killed."

"You've read the police report?"

"It's noted as possible vandalism. However, JDLR was notated on the bottom."

"Not attempted murder?"

"No."

"Well, JDLR is something I guess. I was hoping for more." JDLR means *just doesn't look right* in cop speak. "Didn't they talk to Rudy Lee?"

"He admits that he called Franklin but insisted lights were flashing on and off in the house."

"Franklin and I checked. There was nothing wrong in the house. It was a setup to get me to Wickliffe Manor."

"I've called Rudy and told him the deal was off. I'm going over there today and give him back his money."

"What did he say to that?"

"He threatened to sue again."

"I wouldn't give back his money until he removes

his horses, Hunter. Otherwise, he has no incentive."

"As long as I keep his money, Rudy won't be motivated to leave."

"Start an eviction process."

"I don't want to go public about this. It will make me look bad. You know how people take sides."

"Yeah, usually for the wrong person."

Hunter hung his head. "What a mess this is. I was just getting back on my feet, too." He reached over and hugged me. "I'm sorry about your car. When I make some good money, I'll replace it. You'll have to wait for a time, though. After I return Rudy's money, I'll be broke again."

"What did your insurance company say?"

"They've canceled my policy."

"Isn't that illegal?"

"They accused me of being negligent with the tree and that I didn't tell them about Rudy being a tenant. Informing them about Rudy was on my list of things to do, but I got snowed under and forgot. Now I have to spend the next couple of days looking for a new insurance company."

I glanced at Hunter. His face was haggard and there were dark circles under his eyes. "Today is Sunday. There's nothing you can do until tomorrow. It's a nice day, so let's grill out. Have a nice lunch. Watch an old movie. Take a nap. Relax."

"You make us sound like two old people. Lunch

and a nap. How did we get reduced to that?"

"We *are* old. Let's enjoy our age. Lunch and a nap sound pretty good to me after this week."

"I need to see Rudy and settle this matter."

"Have it your way," I said, sighing. "Off you go, then."

Some people just suck the nice right out of you.

16

I decided to accompany Hunter to Rudy Lee's home. He would need a witness when he wrangled with Rudy, and I intended to tape the conversation, surreptitiously, of course. Hey, no judging. I pay my taxes, follow traffic laws, and have reasonably good manners when out to dinner. That's the best I can do. Everything else is up for grabs.

"I think you should let your lawyer handle this," I said.

"Another bill I wish to avoid."

I made a face, but kept my mouth shut, thinking— how could two very hard-working people such as Hunter and myself always be grappling for money? That's what I wanted to know. I knew most of my money problems were caused by Brannon and his mistress, Ellen Boudreaux, but the buck stopped with me, no pun intended. I should have been more attentive to what was going on with Brannon, but nooooo— I wanted to trust him. Keep my marriage intact and all that rot. What a sap I was. I should have been secretly socking away money and hiring a private detective to follow him. I didn't even know Brannon had sold his business until months afterwards. My thoughts were disturbed when Hunter turned onto Rudy's street, and we encountered a flood of policemen.

One stopped us.

Hunter rolled down his window.

"State your business, sir."

"I'm here to see a man who lives on this street. What's going on?"

"Name." It was not a question, but a command.

"My name is Hunter Wickliffe."

"The name of the person you came to see."

"Rudy Lee."

The officer turned and mumbled something into a shoulder microphone. Someone mumbled back. The officer said to Hunter, "Go on, sir. Detective Drake wants to speak with you."

Yuck. My heart dropped. I had previously encountered this detective, and he was from homicide. He didn't like me, and I didn't like him. "What happened?" I asked, leaning over Hunter to look up at the cop. I don't know why I asked the question because I already knew what had happened. Perhaps something is not real until someone speaks it.

"Yes, why are we being questioned?" Ignoring our questions, the officer motioned Hunter to keep driving down the street until another officer motioned for Hunter to park. "I don't like the look of this," Hunter said, pulling off to the side.

A run-down, beige bungalow with black shutters was cordoned off with yellow crime tape, and we saw a body bag being brought out from the house. The bag was lifted into the back of the coroner's van.

"Is this Rudy's address?" I asked.

Hunter looked at his note with the address written down. "Yep, this is the place."

"If Rudy had so much money, why was he living in such a dump?"

"One of the many mysteries of this entire affair. Look sharp now. We're being summoned."

A plain-clothes cop waved us over. Hunter got out and I remained in the car until the cop waved me over as well. It started to drizzle causing me to pull my jacket up around my neck. The cop motioned us inside the tape.

Hunter grabbed my hand. "Whatever happens, we don't go inside the tape. Understand?" He said to the officer. "I'm a forensic expert. It might disturb the crime scene if we were to step inside the line. We'll wait here."

We hung around for about ten minutes until my left leg started going out. "Hunter, I've got to sit down soon. My leg is twitching."

"Go back to the car. I'll give someone my contact

information and tell them we're leaving."

Just as I started back, Detective Drake emerged from the house and called out to us.

I groaned inwardly.

Hunter whispered, "Don't tell him the story about Lettie Lemore."

He didn't have to tell me that. I knew that story gave me motive. Kill Rudy Lee before he killed me.

Detective Drake pulled his overcoat collar up around his neck against the rain. "Well, well. Look who's here. Josiah Reynolds and Hunter Wickliffe, the two most ghoulish people in the Bluegrass. Let's go down memory lane. Before last Christmas, you, Josiah, found a dead man in the trunk of a car not to mention having found twelve bodies before that. Now, I find you standing in front of the house of another murdered man."

"So, Rudy Lee was murdered?" I asked.

Drake turned to Hunter. "And you, Dr. Wickliffe, had a woman murdered in your house not too long ago."

"Josiah Reynolds has been credited by your own police department as helping to solve all those cases, and I was absolved of any involvement of the murder at my home as you well know."

He replied to Hunter, "Yes, I know about Josiah's cause célèbre about town. It's been lucky she hasn't been arrested."

I said, "You're jealous I beat you to the punch on many of those cases, and you should remember Dr. Wickliffe has been hired to as a consultant for your own department. And it's Mrs. Reynolds to you."

Drake turned to me. "Where were you between eight and ten a.m. this morning?"

"Was that when Rudy was killed? How was he murdered?"

"I'll ask the questions," Drake said, motioning for the coroner's van to take off.

"I was at my farm tending to my animals. As you know yourself, I have a security system that records any comings and goings on my farm, so my alibi is foolproof."

"Will I have to get a court order to view these tapes?"

"I'll be home the rest of the day. Have one of your men come to view the tapes, but you'll need a court order to take them off the property."

"A bit old fashion keeping tapes, isn't it, Josiah? Most people connect their surveillance cameras to their phones now-a-days."

"I'm an old fashion kind of gal. Besides, those tapes come in handy when I have to prove I was at my farm at the time someone was murdered."

Drake jotted down in his notebook. "What about you, Dr. Wickliffe?"

"Got in last night from Las Vegas working on a

case. Got to Josiah's house around ten this morning. Before that, I stopped at a convenience store to get gas and purchased a coffee. The receipt is in my car on the back seat. I know the cashier. She will vouch for me as well. When did Lee die?"

"Unofficially, early this morning." Drake motioned to a man to retrieve the receipt. "Why are you two here?"

Hunter said, "Rudy Lee is leasing my farm for his trotters."

"Since when?"

"Almost a month, maybe."

"And?"

"There was an accident on my farm. We wanted to speak with Mr. Lee if he saw or heard anything."

"That can be taken care of with a phone call."

"I am a trained forensic psychiatrist. Body language is very important. I'd rather see a person eye-to-eye when discussing something as important as an accident."

"You think Mr. Lee was behind this accident?"

"I didn't say that. I just said I wanted to speak with him about it."

"Uh huh," Drake said, pulling out a stick of gum.

"Trying to stop smoking?" I asked.

"What makes you think that?" Drake demanded.

"You have stains on your fingertips from tobacco, and no male over the age of sixteen pops gum unless they are trying to stop smoking. A lot of cops smoke. They have stressful jobs and smoking helps them cope—that or drinking." Under my breath, I said, "or beating their wives."

"Not helping," Hunter murmured.

"When was the last time you spoke to Mr. Lee?" Drake asked Hunter.

"About two weeks ago. He paid his rent, six months in advance. I've been out of town since then on police matters."

Glancing up at the threatening sky, Drake said, "Let's hurry this up. Looks like it's going to rain. And you never had any communication with Lee since?"

"No."

"What about you?" Drake asked, glaring at me.

"Afraid not," I replied.

"Did either of you call to make an appointment with Mr. Lee for this morning?"

Hunter and I shook our heads.

"Why couldn't you wait to speak with Mr. Lee when he came out to your farm?"

"I'm leaving on another case shortly. So we took a chance he might be home. I wanted to get this accident information settled."

Drake said, "Yes, the tree limb hitting Mrs. Reynolds' car."

"That was quick. You know about my car?" I said.

"My men are efficient," Drake replied. "Officer

Riley was only too glad to email us the report. You wanted him to question Mr. Lee about the tree limb."

I asked, "And did he?"

"Mr. Lee said he didn't know what you were talking about. Said the farm was shipshape, and the gates were closed when he left. He thought someone must have been playing a prank."

"A very elaborate prank with deadly consequences," Hunter said. "That's why we are being detained?"

"You're not being detained. I'm asking some friend-ly questions."

I said, "You think we had something to do with Lee's death."

"It crossed my mind," Drake said. "The tree limb story gives you a motive."

"Good thing our alibis are airtight," Hunter commented, fingering his car keys.

"How was Lee killed?" I asked, morbidly curious.

It started to rain in earnest. People were dashing for cover except for us. Ignoring the rain, Drake hurriedly said, "I'll need your contact information, Dr. Wickliffe, for when you leave town. I want to know where you will be and when." He handed Hunter a business card. "You can text me the information."

"Are we still under suspicion? We have rock solid alibis, Detective," Hunter said.

"We'll check your alibis out." Drake looked at me with utter contempt. "And as for you, don't leave town."

I clicked my heels together and gave a crisp salute, saying, "Jawohl, mein kommandant!"

Drake rolled his eyes and went back inside the house.

"No wonder the police hate you," Hunter said. "You antagonize them."

"Not as much as they antagonize me."

"They have a very difficult job. Most police are decent, hard-working chaps. Your own daughter was in law enforcement."

"Look how that turned out."

Hunter said, "Now you're being ridiculous."

"I automatically resist men telling me how to act. It's a knee jerk reaction. Immature, I know."

Hunter and I started back for his car when I spied a newspaper reporter whom I knew. "Go on. I'll catch up," I said to Hunter, before rushing over to speak with my acquaintance.

"Hello, I'm Josiah Reynolds. Do you remember me? We met at Lady Elsmere's Christmas party last winter. It's John something, isn't it?"

"Yeah, it's John Maynard. What are you doing here?"

"May I share your umbrella, John? It's raining cats and dogs. You're a reporter for the local paper."

John Maynard moved over to let me under his umbrella. "You didn't answer my question."

"I met the deceased at Lady Elsmere's fundraiser

for abandoned Thoroughbreds, oh, I say, about a month ago."

"You still didn't answer my question."

"Do you know how Rudy Lee was murdered?"

"Someone used his neck as a pin cushion for a pair of scissors."

"For real?"

"For real," the reporter answered.

"Sounds personal."

The reporter looked amused. "I would say so."

"Have you overheard the police say anything else?"

"How can I? They are in the house."

"Because you have that thingy which enhances sound. I saw it advertised on the internet. When I came over, I saw you put it beneath your coat and take earbuds out, so you must have heard my conversation with Detective Drake."

The reporter smirked. "You are too observant."

"Look, I'm getting drenched, so will you tell me what you heard?"

"What do I get in return?"

"A phone call down the line with a juicy tidbit."

"Quid pro quo, huh?"

"Something of that nature."

"Okay, I'll bite. Mr. Lee was killed between nine and ten this morning. So far, the police haven't turned up anything as most of the neighbors were at church."

"How was the body discovered?"

"Mr. Lee's dog was outside, barking his head off and running around. He's normally a quiet dog, so one of the neighbors thought that strange and gathered up the dog and took him home. Saw Lee's door was opened and went inside. Discovered the body. End of story."

"Was the dog injured?"

"I don't think so, but he did have blood on him. The police think it's Lee's blood."

"Where's the dog now?"

"He's in police custody."

"What kind of dog is it?"

"A lab mutt. His name is Rover."

"You're joking."

"Yeah, I am but I don't think Lee was the imaginative type."

I shook my head. "No, you got it right on the first try. Any suspects?"

"Nada, but they haven't finished canvassing the neighborhood."

I said, "Nothing will turn up. This is a tight-knit neighborhood. These people keep their mouths shut."

"What plays here, stays here?"

"Something like that."

"It's your turn to feed me some juicy tidbits."

"Rudy Lee is from Louisiana. His father was some big shot in the business world. They made their money from sugar. Lee inherited his old man's money and wanted to spend it in Kentucky on horses. He had a heart condition. A bad one."

"That's it?"

"All I got at the moment."

The reporter handed me a business card. "When you get ready to give up something I can sink my teeth into, give me a ring."

"Like what?"

"Like why are you here?"

I laughed. "You already know. You heard everything Dr. Wickliffe and I said to the police."

The reporter grinned. "Wanted to see if your answers would be consistent."

I smiled. "Nice to see you again. Keep in touch."

The reporter smiled. "Oh, I will. You can count on that."

I went over to Hunter's car wondering if I had done the right thing talking to the reporter. I guess I would soon find out.

17

Franklin called me the next morning. "You and Hunter are in the paper this morning."

"Pictures?"

"No, the article is about Rudy Lee. It mentioned you and Hunter were questioned. Looks like Rudy kicked the bucket before you did."

"I'm all torn up about it."

"Lettie Lemore got it wrong."

"Not by much. Rudy is dead, and someone did try to kill me. I'd say she was pretty much on target."

Franklin mused, "We both stuck our feet in that muck without looking. Now, we've got Hunter mixed up in it."

"You can't go around thinking everyone is a complete ass. Hunter needed a tenant on the farm. How were we supposed to know that Rudy would be such a harbinger of doom?"

"At least Hunter got some money out of it."

I asked, "Has anyone claimed his horses?"

"No one has contacted Hunter yet, but it's still early. Rudy's only been dead a day."

"Does the paper say who Rudy's next of kin is?"

"Nope."

"Any suspects?"

"No idea who did it. The police are asking for information."

"They must be hard up then."

Franklin said, "I've got to go to work, but I'll pop around later."

"Gather up Matt and Emmeline. Come to dinner around sevenish."

"See you then." He hung up.

Grabbing a small bag, I called to Baby, and we went outside to check on the chickens. They were chasing bugs and having a grand time. I checked their water and feed inside the coop. No signs of digging around the coop. Crossing my fingers, I opened the flaps to their nesting beds. Low and behold, eggs! Only two, but it was a start. Two lovely small chocolate brown eggs from the Marans. I was happy that my plan was working, and the chickens were calming down.

I trudged into the woods, where I kept a small bowl. From my bag, I poured dog food into it. I had been leaving dog food for the fox to keep her away from my chickens, and it seemed to do the trick! That and the electric fence. I knew I shouldn't feed wildlife, but I hated to see the fox struggle.

Baby sniffed the dog food and turned his nose up at it.

"Ah, too good for the likes of you?" I said. "Here's a treat then. Your favorite." Wagging his tail, Baby looked at me with anticipation as I slipped him a cheese treat which I kept in my pocket. Chowing it down, he nudged me for more and I obliged. Out of the corner of my eye, I saw movement in the bushes, thinking it must be the fox. "Come on, Baby. We need to get home."

Leaving the fox to her own devices, I went about my day, but I kept thinking about Rudy Lee. If Rudy had money, why was he living in such a sketchy neighborhood? And what would have been the motive for Rudy to kill me? None of this made sense. The day went by quickly until I noticed the sun low in the sky. I checked my watch and noticed the hours had gotten away from me. Oops, time to get dinner ready. I put the chickens up and went inside to fix dinner for the lads and the baby.

I emptied several jars of homemade tomato sauce into a pan along with frozen spinach, tiny bits of carrots, and bowtie pasta. Inhaling the fragrance of spices being released from the sauce, I poured in two cups of water and stirred, letting the liquid cook down. Then I made a romaine lettuce salad. Looking at my watch again, I realized I needed to hurry as the boys would be here soon. I popped garlic toast in the oven and heard the front door open.

"Josiah, it's me."

"Hunter, wash your hands and set the table for me, please."

"Just two places?"

"Make it four and get the high chair from the closet."

"Franklin and Matt coming?"

"Yeah."

Hunter came into the kitchen and gave me a kiss on the cheek. "Something smells divine." He lifted the lid from the pot, inhaling deeply.

I turned the stove off. "I need to change my clothes. Can you punt for me?"

"No problem. Listen, Jo. I've brought my bag. I need to leave early in the morning for Las Vegas. I'm still working on that case."

"Sure, you can spend the night." Hunter often spent the night before heading out for an assignment. The airport was closer to my house. I returned Hunter's kiss, but this time on the lips for which he gave my fanny a nice squeeze and a pat to boot.

"Go on, Jo. I'll finish up here."

"Thanks." I undid my apron and tied it around Hunter's waist. As I hurried to my bedroom, I heard a car drive up. Thinking it was Franklin and Matt, I went into overdrive, changing out of my work clothes into nice slacks and sweater combo, combing my hair, and putting on some fresh lipstick. So, it was a shock when I came into the great room and discovered Detective Drake sitting on my blue green mid-century couch sipping coffee served by Hunter. "Detective Drake, to what do I owe the honor?"

"I have some questions before Dr. Wickliffe leaves for Vegas."

"You want to question Hunter?"

"And you as well."

I sat in a chair opposite Drake and watched him glance about the room. He settled on my rotary phone. "Does it work?" He picked up the hand receiver and listened. Surprised, he said, "There's a dial tone. I thought all these phones were unusable."

"The phone company keeps threatening me." I crossed my legs. "I'm having guests for dinner. Can we hurry this along?"

Hunter butted in, "Perhaps, you would like to join us, Detective. Josiah is a fabulous cook."

"Something smells wonderful, but no thank you. My wife is keeping dinner for me."

"I didn't know you were married," I said. "You don't wear a wedding ring."

"Don't like to give the enemy information about my private life."

"We are not the enemy."

"Jo!" Hunter said in a warning tone.

"You don't like the police much, do you, Josiah?" Drake said.

"I like the police fine. It's certain individuals in the police department I can't stand."

Hunter pulled up a chair. "How may we help you, Detective Drake?"

Drake pulled out his notebook. "I want to know why you asked the Woodford County police to talk with Rudy Lee about the incident involving your car at Dr. Wickliffe's farm."

"We told you before. This event has really damaged both Hunter and myself in regards to my car. Mr. Lee called Dr. Wickliffe's brother stating lights were flashing in Wickliffe Manor. Franklin called me to take a look. It would seem only natural that Mr. Lee might have seen something or someone. We wanted to know more about it."

"Why not leave it to the insurance adjuster to handle this matter of damage to your car?"

"Really, now, Detective Drake. Dr. Wickliffe's insurance company canceled his policy."

"Did they?"

Hunter nodded yes.

"Do you both use the same insurance company?"

"No," I said. "I talked with my guy this morning. He said my car had depreciated and the check would be less than I expected, plus my car rental coverage runs out in a week."

Drake said, "I can see that would make a person angry, especially if they suspected a particular person was responsible for the damage."

"I never said anything about anybody being responsible," I replied.

"I talked with Officer Riley who took the report. He thought you intimated Mr. Lee might have had something to do with the accident."

"I never said so. I just asked that he be questioned as to what he saw."

"But you think it?"

My reply to Drake was an icy stare.

"Interesting answer," Drake said. "What about you, Dr. Wickliffe?"

"To be completely honest, we can't rule out the possibility that someone arranged for the limb to fall on Josiah's car. It is strange the gates were left open, the keypad wires had been tampered with, and then the accident. Rudy Lee was the last person on the farm that we know of. Of course, we are curious."

"Do you concur?" Drake asked while looking at me.

"Something's funny. Wouldn't you agree, Detective?" I said.

"Officer Riley had Lee's phone records checked. Lee's phone was not used to call Franklin Wickliffe. He had never called Franklin Wickliffe from his phone ever. Whoever called your brother was not Rutherford Lee."

Hunter and I shot a confused look at each other.

"My brother said the man identified himself as Rudy Lee."

"I don't know what I can tell you, but it wasn't Lee's phone that was used."

Hunter didn't respond.

"I also found it strange that your names were mentioned in the newspaper article about Lee's death."

"I guess I'm to blame," I said.

"What do you mean?"

"I saw a reporter at the crime scene whom I had met at Lady Elsmere's. I went over to talk with him and he remembered me. He told me Rudy was killed by scissors to the neck."

"Now, how would a reporter know this?" Drake asked, perturbed that there might be a leak in his team.

I put on my best innocent face and shrugged. "Was he really killed by a pair of scissors to the neck? Sounds gruesome."

"Since the coroner's report will be released soon, the answer is no. He was not."

Not being able to conceal my surprise, I sat straight up in my chair. "Lee wasn't killed by a pair of scissors?"

With his lip curling up on one side into a smirk, Drake said, "Oh, Mr. Lee was stabbed in the neck all right, but he was stabbed post-mortem."

Well, I'll be jiggered.

18

Franklin poured the wine as I brought the pasta dish to the table. "We passed Detective Drake on the way out."

"He was here asking more questions," Hunter said, taking Emmeline from Matt and putting her in the high chair.

"How did Drake get through the gate?" I asked.

"The gate was opened when I arrived," Franklin said, taking a seat next to Matt.

I sighed. "My horse boarders must have left it open again. What's the point of a security gate if I can't keep it shut?"

Taking a piece of garlic bread, Matt said, "The gate automatically shuts, so he must have tailgated one of the boarders onto the property. There were a couple of cars at the barn when I came home." He pulled little bits of the bread apart and gave them to Emmeline. She tasted one, made a face, and threw the bread on the floor.

"Here," I said, handing Matt a small bowl of cut apples, bananas, and pineapple. "She likes fruit."

"Thanks. Emmy is going through a fussy stage." Matt coaxed Emmeline to eat the fruit, which she enjoyed until she dumped the entire bowl on the floor. Then she started to cry.

Matt looked exasperated. "Sorry, guys."

I asked, "Do you have a bottle?"

"Yes." Matt got up and pulled a bottle from his nappy bag.

"Throw some cereal at her and call it a night," Franklin said, sprinkling parmesan cheese on his pasta.

"Emmy sticks her nose up at store-bought baby food, too. I'm running out of things to try with her," Matt said.

"I doubt she will starve," Franklin said. "She's a plump little dumpling."

"This behavior started about two weeks ago. I never had a problem feeding her before," Matt said, looking worried. He gave the baby her bottle which seemed to soothe her. "Eat fast before she finishes."

"As you said, it's a stage. She'll get over it." I reassured, but I was glad Emmeline was quiet. A crying baby is stressful.

"What did Drake want?" Franklin asked.

"It was a fishing expedition," Hunter said, reaching for the bowl of shredded parmesan. "Leads me to believe we are the only leads Drake has."

"Perhaps we should tell him about Lettie Lemore," I said.

"The story gives you motive, Josiah," Hunter replied. "Makes it seem like you wanted to eliminate Rudy Lee before he did you in."

"But we can prove we were nowhere near Rudy at the time of death."

"You could have paid someone to murder Rudy."

"Nonsense. Where would I get money to pay off a hit man let alone find such a person? It's not like there are hit men running in my social circle."

"Why do you think Drake came to the Butterfly in person? He wanted to see where you lived. What kind of things you had. He was sizing you up. I tell you, Josiah, Drake's gunning for you," Hunter said.

"At least, I never told him anything of importance," Franklin said.

The three of us looked at him.

"He talked to you?" Hunter asked.

"Yeah, the Sunday Rudy died. Tracked me down at my apartment around dinner time."

"What did you tell him?" I asked.

"Just that I had met Rudy at Lady Elsmere's house for a fundraiser and took him home."

Matt asked, "Did you tell him why?"

"Sure. I said he wasn't feeling well. Had heart trouble."

"Is that all you told Drake?" Hunter asked, giving

his brother a stern eye.

"I mentioned that Josiah recommended the farm to him."

"Anything else?" I asked.

"Nope."

"Nothing about Lettie Lemore or the tree accident?"

Franklin looked down at his plate and absentmindedly shoved a morsel of pasta into the sauce.

"Okay, Mr. Loose-lips. Out with the rest," I demanded.

"Now that you mentioned it, I seem to remember confirming that I called you to check on Wickliffe Manor, and a limb had fallen on your car as you entered the grounds, but nothing about the fortune teller." Astonished, Franklin looked around the table. "I SWEAR!"

I asked, "Franklin, where did you take Rudy when you took him home?"

"To that boutique hotel near Gratz Park. I let Rudy off at the front door and watched him go in."

"Did he mention if he was going to rent or purchase a house?"

"Said he had purchased a home in one of those gated communities off Richmond Road near the reservoir and was waiting for the paperwork to go through."

"Did he mention which one?"

"I think he said it was called Trumpet Vine or something like that."

Hunter said, "We went to the address printed on his check. His home was very run down."

"Maybe it wasn't his house," Matt said. "Maybe Rudy was just murdered there."

"Maybe he wasn't murdered at all," I mused.

"The paper said Rudy was killed by a pair of scissors to the neck," Franklin said.

Matt complained, "Do we have to be so graphic around the baby?"

I answered, "She's asleep, Matt. She can't hear a thing."

Indeed, Emmeline has fallen asleep in the high chair. She looked like a little angel.

"Here's the kicker," Hunter said. "Drake said Rudy was stabbed with the scissors post-mortem. I'd be very interested to see the coroner's report. My guess is Rudy died from a heart attack."

"So the case may end up being abuse of a corpse," I said, laughing. "All this trouble due to a man who probably died in his sleep from natural causes."

Hunter chuckled too. "C'est la vie! Or maybe I should say c'est la mort."

I don't know why Hunter and I laughed because we didn't think Rudy's death was amusing. Nervous energy I guess. Rudy was supposed to have murdered me, but I was still kicking and he was dead. One of life's little ironies.

"This runs deeper," Matt said. "Josiah almost gets killed, her car is totaled, Hunter loses his insurance, and someone stabs Rudy Lee after he's dead. I wouldn't shrug this off. You have to be pretty cold to shove a pair of scissors in someone's neck even if they are dead. There's a reason for all of this to be happening."

Leave it to Matt's analytical mind to focus our attention where it belonged.

I switched my line of questioning. "Franklin?"

"Yeeeesss, and I hope this is your last query."

"Did Rudy mention that he had a dog?"

"Nope. Now I have a question of my own. What's for dessert?"

"I have bread pudding warming in the oven."

"I'll serve dessert, hon," Hunter said, rising from the table.

"The plates are on the counter," I said.

Matt mugged at me and Franklin silently mouthed, "Hon?"

I whispered, "Shut up, both of you."

We emitted satisfied groans as we ate heaping spoonfuls of bread pudding until Emmeline awoke and then all hell broke loose. We couldn't get her to stop crying, so Matt took her home. Franklin followed soon after.

I was glad. Emmeline's outburst made me skittish. That's when I knew my nerves were frayed. Otherwise, I would have worked with Emmeline to calm her down.

"Hunter, leave the dishes. I'll clean up in the morning. I'm bushed. Going to bed. You?"

"I'm going to stay in the guest bedroom. I have to get up early in the morning and don't want to wake you. I think we both could do with a good night's sleep."

"Suit yourself. Good night, then." I called Baby, and we went into my bedroom. I locked the steel bedroom door as was my habit and went to bed. The next morning I awoke to a clean kitchen and a note from Hunter stating that he would be home in four days.

Four days! That would give me enough time. Just about. I made a telephone call. "Hello? Yes, it's me. Don't gloat, but I need your help. May I see you?" I looked at my watch. "It's nine now. Ten? Okay, see you then." I hung up.

I needed someone more unprincipled and devious than myself, and there was only one person in town who fit that bill.

The shamus Walter Neff.

19

"Six thousand!" I cried.

Walter sat behind his desk with a grin on his face. He had gained more weight, but at least, he was not wearing a sleazy open throated silk shirt exposing sweaty chest hair with gold chains hanging from his neck. Instead, he was wearing a white button-down cotton shirt, a beautiful silk tie, and pleated pants held up with suspenders. He looked like a country lawyer from the 1940s. I took in his newly appointed office filled with tasteful expensive office furniture along with Paul Sawyier prints hanging on the walls. Walter seemed to be doing okay for himself. "That's what it's going to cost. You're gonna need tech support which I contract out and surveillance around the clock. That doesn't include unforeseen incidental expenses which will be extra. I'm working on other cases which I have to push aside for you. You did say this was to be done immediately—a rush order?"

"Have you forgotten who took care of you after

your heart attack? You lived at my house for months. You should do this for free."

"You threw me out."

"Yes, you ungrateful little turd. You acted as though I was your nurse, maid, and cook."

"You stole my lottery ticket. I could have been rich."

"It wasn't your lottery ticket! It was Ethel Bradley's ticket, and I saved your fanny from going to jail after you attacked her. How many clients would you have if they knew you had tied up a little old lady and threatened to kill her cat?"

"Ah, I was never gonna hurt the old broad. Just wanted to shake her up a little bit." He leaned over. "What about the jewels that were stolen from me? I had them, Jo. I had them in the palm of my hand."

"Liam took the gems. I had nothing to do with that, and again, they weren't yours to keep."

Walter raised his fist. "If I ever see that guy again, I'm gonna push his teeth down his throat."

"Let's put that misdeed in perspective. Again, you were taking something that did not belong to you, and if Liam hadn't been there to steal the gems, you would have died of your heart attack. After all, he did call 911."

"Phooey," Walter said, giving an additional raspberry.

I wanted to punch Walter's fat little perspiring face,

but he had me over a barrel and he knew it. I needed someone with his expertise and his lack of scruples. "Two thousand and not a penny more. That includes everything. No extra expenses."

"Fifty-five hundred."

"Twenty-two hundred in cash. That's all I can afford."

"Cash you say?"

I nodded. "Yes, cash. Your favorite four letter word."

Walter was positively drooling.

"I want everything you can find out about a Lettie Lemore, Zasu Pitts, and a Rutherford Robert Lee from Louisiana."

"Zasu Pitts! What a name."

"I think Lettie Lemore and Zasu Pitts may be one and the same."

"There was a big wheeler dealer by the name of Lee, who hailed from Louisiana."

"That was Rudy's father, but he is deceased."

"How deep do you want me to dig?"

"Far enough to find incriminating tidbits, but not illegal enough that we'll both go to jail if you get caught. As always, should you or any of your Neff Force be caught or killed, my secretary will disavow any knowledge of your actions," I teased.

"Huh?"

"Didn't you ever watch *Mission Impossible* as a kid?"

Walter leaned back in his chair. "We were too poor. Didn't have a TV."

"Don't you ever get tired of lying?"

"Gotta keep my hand in."

"Pictures, credit history, dossiers, police reports—anything you can dig up. If you don't come up with what I need, then no deal."

Walter thought for a moment before standing and extending his hand. "I'll give you two days, Josiah. Not an hour more."

"Deal." I shook his hand.

"Sign here," he said, pushing a contract toward me.

"Walter, do you not understand? We never had this conversation. I was never here."

"Got it, doll face. I'll need an advance though." Walter made a pitiful sucking sound. "For up-front expenses. It is customary."

I rolled my eyes as I pulled three hundred from my wallet. "Get to work, Walter. See you on Wednesday."

I left Walter Neff's office in a lighter mood. Walter might be a sleaze bag, but he knew his stuff.

Now I had to go see a man about a dog.

20

"I'm checking on a dog that was brought in several days ago. His owner, Rudy Lee, died of a heart attack."

"Do you wish to adopt the dog?"

"I'm checking into his welfare. Mr. Lee was a friend of mine," I said.

The Animal Welfare clerk checked her computer. "Do you know the dog's name?"

"I'm sorry, no."

"Can you describe the dog?"

"He was brought in by the police."

The woman looked over her computer at me. "Oh, that dog. He has already been adopted."

"So quickly?"

The woman pushed her glasses back on her nose. "It happens."

"Can you tell me by whom?"

"I sorry, but all adoptions are confidential."

"We're not talking about human babies. We're talking about a dog."

"That is our policy," she said, giving me a steely glare.

Just as I was about to argue with the clerk, the door burst open as an exasperated couple brought in a high strung Irish Setter, which jumped all over the place, knocking things down, and barking loudly. "Please help us!" they cried. "We can't control this animal."

The clerk immediately jumped up and embraced the squirming dog, beckoning to the couple to follow her into the back.

I took this fortuitous opportunity to saunter behind the desk and search for Rudy's dog on the computer. I looked at the date of Rudy's death and found twelve dogs had been brought in that day. One dog was listed with the owner as deceased. That had to be Rudy's dog. I copied down the name and address of the adopter before skedaddling out of the building.

I had another task to perform before I went to the dog's current address. I hurried to the Property Valuation Administrator's office and looked up Rudy's address. Found out he rented it from a Carolyn Stevic. Got her contact info which was a post office box in Shelbyville, Ky. Okay. Let's try the phone number first. I dialed the number on my cell phone. Out of order. A dead end.

I was getting nowhere fast, so I decided to go to the address listed for Rudy's dog as it was in town. Took me twenty minutes to get there as it was on the other side of Lexington near the Meadowthorpe area in an older subdivision with apartment buildings. That was good for me. I wouldn't be noticed as much as tenants move in and out of apartments all the time. I slowly drove around the block and found the house. Two older, four door cars sat in the driveway, which meant someone was home. Since the animal shelter had listed the dog as a part lab and beagle, I was looking for a mutt around thirty to forty pounds.

An older gentleman strolled out of the house with a black and white spotted dog similar to that description. Could I be that lucky? The gods were smiling upon me today. I drove to another street and upon parking the truck, let out my secret weapon—Baby! "Please, Baby, be good. I need to talk to the dog owner. No shenanigans."

Baby tilted his head, trying to understand. He sneezed and licked his nose with that huge tongue of his.

With his leash securely wrapped around my wrist, Baby and I strolled in the direction of the unsuspecting man walking the dog. We ran into him several minutes later, and I stepped aside into the grass with Baby as though courteously giving the man the sidewalk to pass. "Sit, Baby, sit." For once Baby complied, whining excitedly upon seeing the other dog.

"Hello," I said to the passing man.

"A gracious hello to you," he replied, stopping. "My

goodness, that's a big boy you got there. Acts well trained."

I wanted to laugh at the absurdity of Baby being well-trained, but said, "Thank you."

"May I pet him?"

"Sure. He's friendly." I knew if this guy was a dog lover, he would want to pet Baby. Baby is a show stopper. That's why I brought him.

"He's a Mastiff, isn't he?"

I nodded. "English. Who's your friend?" I reached down and let his dog smell my hand, but the dog wasn't interested in me. He was busy sniffing Baby.

"What happened to his eye?"

"A hunter accidentally shot him," I lied.

"That's terrible."

"He does fine. It doesn't slow him down. What about your dog? Looks like he's got some lab in him."

"That's what they told me. Got him from the pound a couple of days ago. They said his owner had died. He's already settled in."

"Nice that you gave him a home."

The older man looked at me with rheumy eyes. "My wife has cancer, and our dog died last month. She felt adrift without a dog in the house, so I went and got her one."

"Why this particular dog?"

"I don't know. We didn't want a puppy, but an older dog who was well-trained. The people at the pound assured me this boy was a good dog. When I went to look at the others, this one just spoke to me. We hit it off right away." The man bent down and fondly patted his dog's head.

"What's his name?"

"He had a collar that said Mr. Joshua with some numbers, so we call him Josh for short. He seems to understand that is his name."

I said, "I guess the numbers were the former owner's phone number."

"Nope. Strange numbers they were. PND 434 followed by nine other numbers. Something like that."

I sighed. There was nothing here but a lonely man walking his new dog. I looked at my watch. "Oh, look at the time. I need to get home. It was nice meeting you. I hope your wife feels better, sir."

"Thank you. My church is praying for her." The man gently tugged on the leash, and the dog reluctantly left Baby to resume his walk.

Baby and I went in the other direction until the gent was out of sight, and we could retrace our steps back to the car.

The mutt was a dead end.

21

I still had the post office box to explore, but the bees needed my attention first, so it would have to be postponed for a couple of days. I had to wait for a warm day when the bees were not huddled in a cluster. Tomorrow would be such a day.

It was early spring, so the bees needed to be checked for food. This was a dangerous time for honeybees for what I called the "starving time" when honey may be low or nonexistent in the hive.

Honeybees in Kentucky make about five hundred pounds of honey a year per hive. I harvest a hundred of those pounds. Perhaps fifty pounds more if the nectar flow is good. To gather the nectar, honeybees literally die from exhaustion. They work themselves to death. The only time they lay down their burden is if the weather is cold when they band together in a ball for warmth. Even then, the bees on the outside of the ball flap their wings to heat the surrounding air and then exchange with other bees for a break. Honeybees are all about work and sacrifice for the hive. There is no such thing as individualism for a honeybee. It is a collective enterprise with one single thought—the hive must survive.

It is this time of the year when bees exhaust their supply of honey and expend more energy looking for non-existent nectar than bringing resources into the hive. This results in a net loss of resources for the hive. Thus a hive can starve to death as they search in vain for food.

I waited until early afternoon when it was the warmest to check on the bees. I usually have Charles' grandson, Malcolm, help me but this was an easy task, so I didn't call him. I pulled out a batch of peppermint sugar patties from the walk-in freezer and made ready to go. The patties are not very nutritious, but have the calories the bees need.

I have fifty hives, so that's five thousand pounds of organic honey since I never allow pesticides on my farm. I sell a pound of honey for over ten dollars and a rare honey for more. I also use nineteenth-century style eight-ounce bottles with cork stoppers sealed with beeswax for gift purchases. I sell those antique-looking honey jars for a pretty penny, especially if they are for a wedding reception. In a good year, I sell Black Locust, Clover, Wildflower, and Buckwheat. I plant the buckwheat and clover. Nature does the rest.

Selecting a bee yard (I have the beehives scattered

all over the farm), I pulled off the top of a hive. Underneath was the inner cover with a hole allowing access to the inner hive. I placed the sugar patty into the hole and placed another one on top of the inner cover. Then quickly, I placed the outer cover back on to keep the heat from escaping. Quick in and quick out. If I don't see the bees at the entrance, I knock on the side of the hive and listen to see if I hear them buzzing. If the bees don't respond, I assume the bees have died. It took me four hours to go through fifty hives. I suspected eight of the hives had died, but couldn't be sure until I could get inside the hive, and I couldn't do that until a really warm day. However, sometimes the bees surprised me and were doing fine all the time.

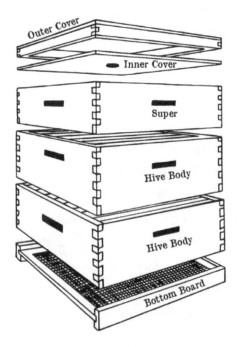

Feeling good about the bees, I went home, took a shower, and changed into fresh clothes. Grabbing a light coat, I went outside to gather the chickens into the coop before checking their water and feed. I searched the nesting boxes and found eggs of the blue and green variety. Things were looking good and maybe by late summer, I could be making a profit with the eggs. At the moment, I was deep in the red and needed to turn this project around. Pleased with the chicken's progress, I gave them a treat of mealworms, which created a frenzied reaction from the chickens. They loved their mealworms.

Since acquiring my hens, I had learned a great deal. Chickens remember faces, know their own names, and will come if called. They can be affectionate, although I hadn't seen any sign of that yet. The chickens tended to ignore me unless they realized I had food, and suddenly, I was their best friend. They seemed to have an affinity for my peacocks, which visited every now and then. They clucked and strutted happily behind horses eating bugs that the horses' hooves stir up.

But the one thing they couldn't abide were canines. Baby was persona non grata with them. They chased him away every time they saw him. I explained to Baby their dislike of him was probably because of the fox. His scent was probably similar. Still, Baby seemed to take the chickens' disdain personally, and it hurt to see his hangdog expression when he trotted over to me after they'd run him off.

I turned on the electric fence and said night-night, even though it was only early evening. I had other things to do like paying bills, but when I walked into the house, I heard my answering machine beeping. Message one was Hunter checking in, saying his case was having issues and he would be home next week—maybe. Message two was Walter Neff stating he had information and wanted to see me pronto. I called him back.

"Whadaya have?"

"Goodies. Lots and lots of goodies," Walter said.

"I can hear you glowing on the other end of the phone."

"I need to see you."

"Can it wait until morning?"

"Okay, but our pigeon might fly away."

"Tell me over the phone if it's that important."

"No way. This deserves the personal touch. I want to see your face when I tell you."

"It must be bad news then."

"Let me come over. I haven't had a home cooked meal in the longest time."

"Who said anything about dinner? You are shameless, Walter."

"You have to eat. I have to eat."

"Take me out to dinner then. *I am the client.*"

"But you're such a good cook, and I miss your cooking."

The truth was I hardly cooked any more. I can't stand for long periods of time without resting, and that is hardly the scenario when one is preparing a cheese souffle or churning peach ice cream. My business partner, Eunice, saves unused meals from wedding receptions for me and stores them in the walk-in freezer. You'd be surprised by the number of people who don't show up for receptions, and the wedding party refuses to be bothered with the leftovers. The amount of food we give away to the staff, plus what Eunice and I consume is astounding, but nothing goes to waste. Anything we can't eat, Eunice takes to a women's shelter. Since she and I can't stand to look at another ambrosia salad, off it goes to feed women in need. I hear it is a very popular dish at the shelter.

"Okay, Walter, but once I've fed you, the meeting is over. You go home."

"Be there soon." Walter hung up.

Fool me once, shame on you. Fool me twice, shame on me. I must have a bullseye on my back where Walter Neff is concerned.

Irritated with myself that I let Walter bamboozle me yet again, I pulled two mahi mahi steaks out of the freezer and put them in the oven. After making a salad, I threw two russet potatoes in the microwave and steamed some broccoli. After washing a carton of strawberries, I left a small cheesecake on the counter to warm up before setting the table, changed my clothes, and brushed my hair. I was exhausted. Even an easy meal like the one I had prepared for Walter was soon to be a thing of the past. I just didn't have the stamina anymore.

Grabbing a notepad and pen, I waited patiently for Walter, only to jump when the microwave dinged the potatoes were done. I had no idea why I was nervous. Walter had to have bad news.

Otherwise, why would he insist on seeing me to-night?

22

"No wine?"

"Walter, please. Can we get on with your report?"

"If you insist." Walter pulled out a manila envelope and dumped its contents on my coffee table.

"What am I looking at?"

"This is a picture of Lettie Lemore," Walter said, holding up a photograph.

"Taken this year at the Keeneland Horse Sales. Probably there to drum up business for her horse whispering gig."

"Okay."

"Look closely. Tell me what you see in the background."

I took the picture and held it close to my face, looking at the people in the background. Since it was the horse sales at Keeneland Race Course, the aisles were packed. It took me a while to find him. I pointed at a face in the crowd. "This is Rudy Lee."

"Yes, it is."

"So? They were both at the horse sales."

"Rudy Lee claimed he was interested in Standard-bred horses. This is a Thoroughbred horse sale."

"Horse people go to all sorts of horse sales, and people go to Keeneland to rub elbows and be seen."

"Take a closer gander at Mr. Lee's expression and what he is looking at, doll baby."

I peered closer. "From this angle, he is smiling at Lettie, but her back is to him."

"Not completely. She's in profile, so he would have had a good look at her. Weren't you under the impression Mr. Lee had never met Lettie Lemore before Lady Elsmere's party?"

"That's the inkling I got but he never really said. Where did you get this?"

"From your friend, John Maynard, the reporter for the local paper. He said he spoke to you on the day of Rudy Lee's death outside the man's home."

"That's true. He mentioned my name in his article about the death the next day."

"Maynard has a keen interest in Lee's death. He thinks Mr. Lee was murdered."

"But the coroner has ruled Lee died of a heart attack. John Maynard even wrote about the coroner's decision in the paper." I didn't mention the scissors, wondering if Maynard had discussed that with Walter. The scissors were never mentioned in the paper.

"I talked to Maynard at length, and he has quite the file on this case."

"Why is he so interested?"

"Maynard is from Louisiana and knew of the Lee family. He even crossed paths with Rudy Lee."

"He's quite a bit younger than Lee. I doubt they would run in the same social circles."

"It comes closer to home than that. Maynard had a relative who died from a hit and run accident twenty years ago in Louisiana. From witness statements, the police confirmed the driver was Rudy Lee, but no charges were ever brought before the grand jury."

"Lee was never charged at all?" I asked.

"Nope. He claimed his car was stolen hours before the accident, and he had an alibi the police couldn't shake. He was in a hotel room with—" Walter's voice trailed off.

"Let me guess. Lettie Lemore."

Walter slapped his knees. "Give the woman a cigar."

"Jumping Jehoshaphat! What else?"

"Maynard gave me a copy of the coroner's report for Lee."

"How did he get a copy of it? It's not public yet."

"Same way I got a copy from him. Greasing the palm."

"Maynard wanted money? Not revenge?"

"They are one and the same with Maynard."

I perused the report. "I don't understand this. It says Lee had no heart disease. Cause of death is undetermined. Makes no sense." I looked up. "I know the man had heart trouble. Lee had an episode right before my eyes, and I gave him a nitroglycerine tablet from his own pocket."

"I've looked at the police inventory. There was no medication found in his home or on his person. The police called the pharmacies in the Bluegrass and Louisville. No one reported filling a prescription for a Rutherford or Rudy Lee."

I leaned back in my chair. "This whole thing smells."

"Most likely you gave him a sugar pill. Did you look at the prescription bottle?"

"No, I was too busy trying to get that child proof cap off the bottle. Lordy, I hate those things. Why did Maynard write that Lee had died of a heart attack if the report says cause of death is undetermined?"

"Maynard has a theory about what happened."

"Want to share it with me?"

"He wouldn't tell me, but I think he is trying to ferret the killer out."

"So Maynard doesn't think Lee died from natural causes?"

"No, and I gather neither do the police, but they can't prove anything."

"Hmm."

"I did some digging based on what Maynard told me."

"And?"

"Rutherford Robert Lee was a wastrel. His addiction was gambling. His father couldn't stand him, and after he shelled out a substantial amount to settle large gambling debts to keep his son's knees from being broken, the old man cut Rudy Lee out of his life."

"Was this common knowledge?"

"No, Lee was allowed to live in a small cottage on the family property for free and use his father's company vehicles, but he never stepped inside his father's house again. Even on his deathbed, Lee's father refused to see him and gave the rest of his money to charities."

"What about the old man's business?"

"It was bought out in a hostile takeover by a competing company, and Rudy Lee was left with nothing, having gone through all his assets by then."

"The man lied about everything and I fell for it, hook, line, and sinker."

"This ain't your first rodeo, Toots. You should have known better."

"You're right, Walter. No use crying about it now. What's our dead guy's connection with Lettie Lemore?"

"Besides being lovers?"

I couldn't help but wince. "I don't get it. Lemore's a lovely woman. Why would she tie herself to Rudy Lee, who's been on a slippery slope for years? And then there's the age discrepancy. She must be about thirty years younger. I don't see the sexual connection."

Walter pulled out two photographs and held them up for me to see.

"That's Lettie Lemore in a mug shot."

"Correctomundo, but it's under her alias of Carolyn Stevic."

I smiled inwardly as I didn't let on that I already knew Lettie Lemore was Carolyn Stevic.

"She owned the house Rudy Lee was living in. She owns lots of property in three states—Kentucky, Louisiana, and upstate New York near the Canadian border."

I said, "Could they be safe houses on the north and south borders of the country with Kentucky in the middle as a rest stop?"

"Louisiana does not share a border with Mexico."

"I'm aware of that fact, Walter, but with a boat Lemore could head out into the gulf for Mexico or any island in the Caribbean."

"I'll give you that."

"What was Lemore charged with?"

"In this mug shot, she was charged for larceny and fraud."

"How many other aliases does she have?"

Several, but Zasu Pitts is her real name."

I picked up the mug shot. "She looks very young."

"She's a career criminal. Eighteen in this picture."

"What happened to the charges?"

"Dropped as were the other fifteen charges against

her during her time in Louisiana."

"I take it Louisiana is her home state?"

Walter nodded. "She met Lee in a gambling joint while dealing blackjack when she was eighteen. She knew how to pluck this pigeon's feathers with sex and money to feed his gambling habit."

"Why would Lemore give him money?"

"In exchange for information. Lee knew everyone and his connections were valuable. With him backing her, she could elevate herself higher into society."

"As what?"

"An assistant. Long lost daughter. Kissing cousin. Who knows?"

"Did she come directly to Kentucky from Louisiana?" I asked, rummaging through the other pictures and documents.

"She spent a couple years in Vegas."

"Dealing blackjack?"

"By this time, she had a magic act."

"Don't tell me. She predicted people's fortunes by touching a personal object of theirs."

"And people say you're a dumb redhead."

"Lemore keeps a post office box in Shelbyville."

"How do you know this?"

"Matt went to see Lemore at her office and noticed mail addressed to Carolyn Stevic at this post office address."

"You want me to check it out?"

"I'll take care of it. I don't feel like paying you to drive to Shelbyville."

Walter twisted his bottom lip.

Ignoring his pouting, I asked, "Have the police made the connection between Lettie Lemore and Rudy Lee?"

"I'm sure John Maynard has made them aware of the connection. There's just one problem though."

"Yeah? What's that?"

"Lettie Lemore has vanished from the face of the earth!"

23

I parked on another street and walked to Lettie Lemore's house as the borrowed truck would be out of place in this ritzy neighborhood. However, I looked the part. I was wearing my black funeral/cocktail dress, pearls, and a nice overcoat, complete with polished shoes, gloves, nice handbag, and oversized sunglasses. It's amazing that a woman in a dress is considered non-threatening and dismissed by people. And if the neighbors were to ask me why I was breaking into Lemore's swanky house, I would answer that she was putting the house up for sale and I was the realtor. Fortunately, no one questioned me as I went to the back of the house and used my credit card to jimmy the lock on the kitchen door.

Stepping inside, I called out in case someone was present. I didn't want to get shot for breaking and entering, which I would deny to my dying day if the police should chance upon me. I listened, but no one answered and no footfalls sounded. Confident no one was in the house, I opened a door leading from the kitchen. It led to a staircase going to a dark basement. No way was I going down there. I closed the basement door and locked it. Thinking that might not be enough, I wedged a kitchen chair under the doorknob—just in case. I've watched my share of scary movies. You can never know what may be lurking in the bowels of an old house.

Leaving my handbag on the kitchen counter, I pulled my stun gun from my pocket and began to search the house. The furniture was tasteful but modest with neutral colors throughout the house with grays, beiges, and chocolates dominating. The house seemed masculine to me rather than feminine, and the choice of décor was bland for a person with such a flamboyant personality. Yeah, that was it. The house was impersonal. No sign of a pet. Not even one plant. Nothing to care for. No pictures. Clean and utilitarian.

It didn't take me long to find an office on the first floor. This was the only room so far that spoke of Lemore's personality. She was a prolific reader. One wall was lined with books. I gave the books a passing glance as I headed to the desk. Yippee!

Lemore had a massive antique desk just begging for me to riffle through it. I went through the desk drawers and after finding nothing, I pulled them out and tipped them over. Nothing taped underneath or on the backside. Drats!

Most people hid things in their desk because it was convenient. I crawled into the desk's kneehole and searched, tapping the wood to see if a hidden drawer might pop out. Lemore was a magician of sorts. She wouldn't think like ordinary people, and a secret drawer would not be out of the question. Nothing.

Down but not defeated, I sat in Lemore's office chair. My leg was starting to throb. I was getting too old for this kind of gig and dreaded going up the staircase to Lemore's bedroom and search. After an office, the bedroom is the second most searched room. I should have let Walter Neff search the house, but why let him have all the fun? But much to my surprise, I wasn't having fun.

Even if I had wanted Walter to search the house, I couldn't afford him anymore. After I paid Walter his blood money, I was broke until the next market day. Walter doesn't take IOUs. So it was up to me to push the agenda further.

My stomach growled. Clutching my tummy, I ignored my hunger pains and tried to think of what to do next. I couldn't believe the house was clean. I mean clean in the sense no clues were left behind. Lemore must have forgotten something incriminating. If the house didn't pan out, I would have to break into her office. Two breaking and enterings in one day. That was a bit much even for me. I hoped I would find something upstairs.

Sitting in the chair, I contemplated my next move. While gaining the energy to tackle the stairs, I studied the bookcase across from the desk. The bookcase was straight across from her desk. Lemore was a reader of biographies, bodice-ripper romances, magic, and the occult. She had a constant view of the bookcase when sitting at her desk. Perhaps, Lemore was not different than everyone else. People like to hide things where they can keep an eye on them. If I were Lettie Lemore, I would probably hide something in the books. Perhaps there was a safe behind them. I bypassed the romance books. They were paperbacks and too small to hide anything significant. I went straight to the large hard-back biographies. I pulled them out and flipped through the pages. Again, nothing. No secret maps, no confessions, no bank books, and no hidden safes.

I rummaged through the occult books. Then I saw it. A black book with gold printing on the spine—Liber AL vel Legis. I took in a sharp breath. Lemore was into serious stuff. Liber AL vel Legis is commonly known as the Book of the Law, written by warlock Aleister Crowley. I'm talking about a real serious dude dabbling in *black magick*. Not that I believe in such nonsense, but just in case, I made sure my gloves were on tight before I pulled the book out. I didn't want it touching my skin.

Lemore had notes in the margins written in pencil, but all of it had to do with the spellbinding—not murder. Disappointed, I put the book back when I noticed something glinting on the back of the shelf. I reached up and felt around. My hand caught something and as I clasped my fingers around it, I heard the front door open. I think my heart stopped. Who was it that had come into the house? Was it Lemore returning? Oh, golly, I had to get out of there!

I thrust my find in my pocket and slid against the wall, looking into the hall mirror. My heart was beating a mile a minute. The reflection in the mirror showed none other than John Maynard. I almost fainted. How would I be able to explain my presence if he found me? Hey, wait a minute! What was Maynard doing here?

I tiptoed to the office closet where Lemore stored supplies and slowly closed the door, leaving it ajar just enough to peek at Maynard when he came into the room. He must have come for the same reason I had. I watched him rummage through the desk and grow more exasperated when he found no computer or personal files. He pulled the books from their shelves and left them in a rag tag fashion on the floor, except for Lemore's Liber AL vel Legis. He searched the book as I had and read some of her notes, finally putting the book in a satchel he had brought with him. Scratching his head about where to look next, he went through the rest of the downstairs and then climbed the stairs taking two at a time.

My search was over. I had to get out undetected as Maynard was feeding the police information. I certainly didn't want Detective Drake to know I'd been snooping around. Taking off my shoes, I put them in my coat pocket. After I had eased from the closet and was creeping to the back door, one of my shoes fell, making a loud thudding upon the wood floor. I froze and looked up at the ceiling, wondering if Maynard was going to bounce down the stairs.

A toilet flushed upstairs. Seeing this was my getaway cue, I retraced my steps out the back door and slunk near the side of the house in case Maynard looked out the upstairs windows. He might see movement, but he wouldn't see me in full. I quickly slipped on my shoes and crossed the front of Lemore's neighbor's yard. I knew Maynard wouldn't be able to see me from that angle. If perchance, he did come out on the porch, Maynard would see the back of a nicely dressed woman with black hair calmly walking down the sidewalk. He wouldn't mistake me for Lemore as she was much shorter than I.

I got back to the truck and jumped inside before pulling off my wig and throwing on a plaid shirt. I would check my coat pockets later. Right now, I needed to get out of Louisville, find a bathroom, and have a drink. The bathroom seemed to be a more urgent need at the moment.

Talk about messing one's unmentionables.

24

Several days later I got home from the market and found Hunter's car was in the driveway. I hurried inside to find Hunter nursing a drink on the patio. It was cold and I shivered when joining him. "Hunter, come inside. What are you doing out here? It's freezing."

"I let myself in. Hope you don't mind."

"Of course not. Come on. Let's go inside and I'll light a fire." He followed me inside and watched me while I lit a fire in the stone fireplace and made a pot of hot tea. After pouring myself a cup, I joined him on the couch. "Now, isn't this more comfy?"

"Yes, quite."

"Why are you back? I thought you were still working on a case in Vegas."

"I was but I got sacked."

"Whatever for?" I asked, alarmed.

"Actually, I was asked to recuse myself, so I did. I also returned the entire consulting fee."

"Oh, dear! Hunter, you've worked on that case for

months. You gave all that money back?"

"It was the right thing to do, Jo." He grimaced. "Every time I think I'm getting back on my feet financially, the rug is pulled out from underneath me. So frustrating."

"What brought this about?"

"These." Hunter took out his phone and showed emails to the Las Vegas Police concerning the death of Rudy Lee. "Someone was sending these to a reporter in Las Vegas who shared them with the police."

The mentalist is the key and her henchman presents the lock.

I scrolled down.

Do as thou wilt. She does.

I scrolled more.

The key has gone to the falls to work for the kingfisher.

"Apparently the Vegas police found a connection between Rudy Lee and the murder I was hired to analyze."

"Can you tell me about this case now?"

"The Las Vegas Vice Squad has been investigating a drug cartel working out of Vegas for three years. They know drugs are being smuggled to the east coast, but they haven't discovered how."

"Wouldn't it have been more prudent to work the

west coast? It's much closer."

"The police think this cartel has discovered a new distribution route to the northeast coast. They got their big break in the case when a Johnny Stompanato was murdered behind the Blue Heron Casino."

"Who was Johnny Stompanato?"

"He was a lieutenant from another cartel, which specializes in distribution. We're not talking about pot here. We're talking about real nasty stuff being peddled to kids."

"The middle man."

"Precisely. The police think he was there to negotiate a deal with someone working at the Blue Heron. The police thought drugs were being smuggled into the Blue Heron and then moved through the supply route until they reached Canada with stop offs in between."

"Maybe someone didn't like Stompanato's terms."

"Or Stompanato said nada to the deal and walked away. We don't know."

"Whom did he meet?"

"There is surveillance video showing him playing craps in the casino, having a few drinks at the bar, and then entering an elevator which connects with a walkway to the adjoining hotel. After that we lost him for twenty-five minutes until we see him walk through the casino again and ask for his car at the back of the Blue Heron."

"The valet service was at the back of the casino?"

"Walk-ins off the strip come through the front door. Guests arriving in taxis, buses, limos, and personal vehicles enter through the back entrance."

"The police have no idea with whom Stompanato met? Hotels usually have cameras everywhere."

"The police do, but I'm not at liberty to say who."

"What do you think went down?"

"Stompanato was killed in a hit and run. Witnesses said Stompanato was waiting at the entrance for his car when a vehicle approached at high speed and deliberately swerved at him. Two witnesses took down the license plate number. The problem is with that."

"Are they similar plate numbers?"

"Very. Only one digit differs, but all the witnesses agreed on the make and color of the car."

"Let me guess. The driver was apprehended, but he has an alibi. The car was stolen from a solid citizen, and the driver has no connection with it."

"The driver was identified as Gerry Harl via the casino's security cameras, but any good lawyer can discredit the security camera footage. The ID is not a hundred percent as the video is pretty low resolution. It would cause doubt in some jurors' minds."

"If the police believe they have caught their man, why did they hire you?"

"I've been working on this case off and on for almost a year. I was initially hired to view the crime scene and review the security video. I came to the conclusion as did the Vegas police that Stompanato's death was murder and not a random hit and run accident. Then I was asked to watch the taped interviews of the driver's interrogation to look for any inconsistencies. The driver still maintains it is mistaken identity, and the police can't shake his alibi."

"If they can't shake the man's alibi, then the police must have the wrong man."

"I don't think so. I can't go into specifics but I was to provide a deposition next week as to why I think the police have the correct man. The problem is that they can't directly tie the man to the casino, but they can tie him to an employee who worked there."

I interrupted, "Lettie Lemore."

"Gerry Harl was a former boyfriend, but Lemore is considered a weak link as she left Las Vegas and came to Kentucky almost a year ago. As far as the police are concerned, she has no connection to this case. Also the police checked and the two have not had any communication with each other months before the murder or since the perp has been arrested."

"I take it the man's phone and computer records have been checked."

"Yep, and nothing was found. Just a few snapshots of when the two dated. Even that was loosey goosey. You know—friends with benefits kind of thing."

I thought for a moment. "Hunter, what is the conviction rate of court cases in which you testify?"

"Ninety percent there about."

"How soon would anyone have known you were hired via the police?"

"I don't think a couple of days would pass before it would become common knowledge. I have a national reputation, and my picture has been in papers, so it would be easy to identify me. I give out my business cards to witnesses. Detectives working the case and reporters who work the crime beat would know within hours."

"Who hires you?"

"Sometimes it is a police department and sometimes, like this Las Vegas case, the DA's office hired me."

"Were you going to testify this was a murder for hire that implicates top management of the Blue Heron Casino?"

"I'm not at liberty to discuss that. I signed a non-disclose contract."

"Why must you be mum about that? You're opening up about other things."

"I can speak only of general items that have already been stated in the Vegas media. I can't go into specifics of the case."

"It would seem to me the police should try to get this perp to roll over on who gave the order for Stompanto's death."

"They were hoping that by forcing a trial it would

lead to the big boys. A deal is still on the table."

"The perp is betting that he is going to win this trial and keep his boss' identity safe."

"I think that's what is going on."

"Okay. When did Lemore quit the Blue Heron Casino?"

"In April of last year."

"When were you hired?"

"February of last year."

"I see."

"What are you getting at, Josiah?"

"I assume the car was found and checked for fingerprints."

"It was. The car had indeed been stolen, but the perp's fingerprints were not found in the car. Neither was his DNA."

"Your testimony is crucial to the case then."

"Yes, I'm afraid the rest is circumstantial at best."

"Did any of the witnesses identify him as the driver?"

"Yes, but you know how witnesses ID's are. They aren't considered as reliable as forensic evidence."

"You've got a perp that has an alibi, a car with none of his DNA or prints, and surveillance footage that doesn't a hundred percent identify him."

"We know the car is the one used to kill Stompanato. His blood and hair were found on the hood. We have witnesses who identified the driver, we have surveillance footage of the murder, and the suspect failed his polygraph test."

"The polygraph test is not admissible in court which is why you were brought in."

"Listen, I'm beat and this is beginning to feel like I'm in court. Too many questions."

Taken aback, I merely said, "You still haven't told me why you were canned. What do those emails have to do with you?"

"It has to do with the police report about the tree limb incident. The police report states you wanted Rudy Lee questioned in regard to the incident, and Rudy Lee was an associate of Lettie Lemore who is a known past girlfriend of the defendant. It throws shade on the case. My association is a liability now."

I finished for him. "The police think Lemore's quitting the Blue Heron after you were hired and coming to the Bluegrass is suspicious."

"Undoubtably. No one will hire me if this gets out. It will harm my reputation."

"How? You are the victim here."

"It means that I can be gotten to, Jo. I can be threatened. Don't you see? This was a long con using my home and my girlfriend to threaten me off the case. I'm so stupid I didn't see the connection."

I could see what the problem was. Hunter was losing his confidence. He was afraid that he was not at the top of his game and was putting people he loved in jeopardy. That's Hunter. When he gets frightened, he lashes out.

"Hunter, I can see you are wiped out. Lie down on the couch and let me make dinner. A quick nap and some food in your belly will make the world seem better. I promise you things will look brighter in the morning."

I felt sorry for Hunter. With the stress of this case and his financial problems, Hunter was showing signs of acute anxiety and depression. I knew if Hunter would sell Wickliffe Manor, he could live a lavish lifestyle, but he was like me in that regard. We were both trying to save the land from the bulldozer.

He had the money from Rudy Lee's lease, which would tide him over for a while, and there was the question of his horses and trotting equipment. As Lee had died intestate, Hunter could appeal to the courts for those horses. Whether or not a judge would award Hunter's claim of Lee's property was another matter. I'm not sure what the law was regarding inheritance in this matter.

Hunter lay down on the couch as I put an album of Beethoven's piano sonatas on the record player before making a quick meal. I heated up some leftover lasagna and made a quick salad. When I went to check on Hunter, he was fast asleep and snoring. I gently covered him with an afghan and turned off the lights.

My leg was hurting, so I wanted to take a little pill to

chase the boogeyman away. You might think I'm a hypocrite when I have illegal pain pills squirreled away in my safe, but the way I think about it, there is a big difference between heroin, crack, and meth. Of course, that could be the junkie in me talking. All of these drugs were taken to push away pain. Every kind of pain. I understood the desire to flee from pain by any means. I hoped God understood as I knew Hunter would never. That's why I never told him about my little stash. I realized before Hunter and I could move on to the next level in our relationship, I was going to have to give up my hoard of ill-gotten pills. That was going to be hard.

I took my meal into my bedroom where Baby was already ensconced with the Kitty Kaboodle. I turned on Hitchcock's *Rebecca* with Joan Fontaine and Laurence Olivier until I, too, slept the sleep of the dead.

25

Hunter was gone when I awoke. He had a lot of things to work out, so I didn't call him. I knew what he was going through. I had been through it myself.

Hunter thought he was a failure and his confidence was at an all time low. He was a middle-aged man with several failed marriages and a rundown estate which was sucking both his money and energy. And now this dismissal from an important case. The only shiny penny in Hunter's life was his job. If Hunter could not prevent his sterling reputation from being tarnished, he was ruined. And Hunter was right, even though he was innocent of any impropriety. It only took a whiff of a bad odor to taint someone in Hunter's position.

The best thing I could do at the moment was stay out of his way and offer support when asked. So I went about my day. I let the chickens out, filled up the water troughs in all the pastures, and checked my beehives. The day was warm so the bees were out collecting pollen from maple trees, a staple food of bees besides honey.

Once the days became warmer, I would go through the hives and look for a frame with queen cells. I would take that frame out with several other frames of bees and create additional hives. The new queen would hatch and emerge, flying out to mate with drones high in the trees. If she mated successfully, the queen would return to her new hive and begin laying eggs. It was a dangerous trip for her and not all queens make it home. I ordered extra queens from a queen breeder just in case, but I liked to use my own breeding stock whenever possible.

The hives looked good, so I headed home, picking up the mail on my way back. Going through the mail, I noticed a letter from the insurance company! I tore the envelope open. They had settled and enclosed was my check for the Prius. Oh, dear, it was less than I thought it would be. No use arguing with them. I needed to formulate a plan of action regarding transportation. Suddenly, I had a thought.

I drove to an old barn where I stored odds and ends, including my treasured old VW van. When I had been recuperating in Key West, Matt had some work done on it, but I got the Prius and forgot about it. I couldn't keep Charles' truck forever and needed reliable transportation that could convey my goods to and from the market. Maybe the VW was the ticket. It all depended on how decrepit it was.

There it was. Right where I had left it. I pulled off

the tarp and spoke softly. "Hello, old friend. Remember me?"

The driver's door squealed and protested as I tugged it open. The van smelled musty. Thank goodness there was a handle to grab or I never would have been able to heave myself up otherwise. The key was in the ignition. With fingers crossed, I turned it. Nothing. The battery must be dead. I wondered what else was wrong with the old gal. I checked the rest of the van. The inside looked okay—not great, but okay. I had always taken good care of the upholstery. It needed a few tweaks here and there, but seemed to be in fair condition for the most part. One half of the windshield was missing and it needed a paint job on the outside, but otherwise, it looked okay. Perhaps I could get the van running again.

I got out and pulled the tarp back in place before patting the side. "Don't worry, girl. I'll be back." Reinvigorated, I got into the truck and drove over to the equipment barn on Lady Elsmere's farm. Getting out, I had to duck and sway as men were busy pushing a hay baler into the shop and running back and forth to the equipment storage shed for parts. This was where Lady Elsmere had all her business and recreational vehicles maintained and refitted. It was located at the back of her farm, so the neighbors heard very little noise and vehicles could only be moved from the barn after dark unless needed on the farm. She also loaned out her mechanics which garnered goodwill from the neighborhood and kept the complaints down.

I was on a mission to poach one of her mechanics myself. I went into the office, which opened to the main shop floor. The place was abuzz with activity as men of all sizes and shapes, bent over the entrails of farm implements and trucks. They bantered about their old ladies and groused about taxes while discussing whether to repair or replace a blown engine. The shop manager barked orders at his guys as he moved about the cavernous enclosure, swilling a large mason jar of cold sweet tea. The palpable level of testosterone almost bowled me over.

A small man with thick wavy black hair looked up from his desk. His face lit up as he recognized me. Jumping up, he came over. "Mrs. Reynolds, are you returning the truck?"

"Not yet, Jackson. I've come to ask another favor."

"How can I help?"

"I need someone to get my VW van running."

Jackson blurted out, "That old thing." His eyes widened after seeing the disappointed look on my face. "Pardon me. I meant no disrespect."

I laughed. "No problem. It just throws me when people refer to my van as ancient. It was the car of my youth, so that means I must be old, too." I sighed. There was no getting around it. Both my VW and I had seen better days.

"Let's ask the fellows. Somebody may be interested. What are you offering?"

"Top dollar. Whatever they are making here."

"Her Ladyship pays us good money. More than shops in town."

"That's because Lady Elsmere wants the best."

Jackson beamed at my praise. "Okay. Let's ask."

I followed him into the main work area.

"Hold it down, guys. I've got a proposal from Mrs. Reynolds, so listen up."

The men put their tools down and turned toward me.

"Hi, I'm Josiah Reynolds. I live next door. Many of you know me. I have a 1966 VW van that I want restored in the next couple of months. I will pay what you make here."

"Does it run?" one man asked.

"I don't know. I know it needs a new battery. It won't turn over."

"When was the last time it was started?"

"It's been years now."

The men scoffed. "Are you sure you want to invest in such an old clunker? It might cost thirty thousand dollars to restore it."

"I can't spend that much. Nowhere near that. I'm not interested in cosmetics. I just need it to run."

The men went back to work one by one. It was clear they were not interested in rehabilitating my van.

"I'll do it," a voice chirped up.

Jackson and I bent our heads around the various men who were also turning to see who had volunteered.

A young woman stepped out from beneath a battered old Land Rover perched on a lift. She wore grimy mechanic's coveralls. There was grease on her face and hands, and dark hair cascaded down her back in a long braid. "I'll do it."

"Have you ever worked on such a vehicle before?" I asked.

"No, but I've always wanted to work on a classic. Ask around. These boys will tell you I'm qualified."

"I'm asking you."

"I'm good, better than some of these NASCAR wannabes."

Some of the men threw good natured insults at her. She waved them away.

I glanced at Jackson, who nodded his approval. "Come into the office and we'll settle this."

The girl followed, sticking her tongue out at the other mechanics.

I asked, "What's your name?"

"Renata Gomez."

"How old are you?"

"Twenty. Listen, would you be asking a guy this stuff?"

"Actually, I would."

The girl twisted her lips. "I like older cars, and yours may be what I'm looking for. One day I want to open my own shop and restore classics."

"Big dream."

"My father always said dream big or stay home."

"I want this car to be dependable. Nothing fancy. I only have so much money to spend on it."

"What condition is it in?"

"Lots of rust on the outside and some rot in the upholstery, but nothing drastic. Never mind what it looks like. I just need you to get her running."

"Does it have a split windshield?"

"Plus the five windows on each side."

"Those bodies are very hard to find nowadays. You could sell the body alone for a profit as is. What are you going to use it for?"

"I drove it as a work vehicle for decades. It was the most dependable vehicle I've ever owned. My father gave it to me as a wedding gift. It had been his, so it has great sentimental value to me."

"How much are you prepared to spend?"

"Your hourly wage up to 100 hours."

"If I get her up and running like new, I'll want a bonus."

I inhaled quickly, wishing I had had this girl's confidence and guts when I was her age. "Let's see if you can get her to start before we talk about bonuses."

"I'll get her going. She'll purr like a kitten."

"Okay. Jackson seems to think you can handle this, so I'll give it a go."

"Where's the van now?"

"In a barn on my place."

"I'll come by after work. Some of the guys will help me tow it back here."

"Sounds like a plan. Come through the side pasture gate and watch out for my animals. They have free access on the farm."

The girl nodded and looked at Jackson.

"That's all, Renata. Go back to work now."

Once Renata went back into the workshop, I asked, "Am I making a mistake here."

Jackson shrugged. "Renata's ambitious and knows her stuff. What she doesn't know, she'll ask for help."

I looked at my watch and had to get back to the Butterfly. It was time for Baby's tinkle break.

"Thanks, Jackson. Appreciate your help."

"Sure, any time. Hope it works out for you both."

I hurried home where Baby met me at the door with a reproachful look as he rushed out to do his business. I waited at the door until he had finished. "Come on, Baby. Haven't got all day."

Baby took his time, sniffing the truck tires, clumps of grass, and then sat down to wash himself. But I had the upper hand. All I had to say was, "TREAT!" and Baby came running. I shut the door snugly after him. After giving Baby a peanut butter snack, I went into my office and studied all the information Walter Neff had procured for me. I really hadn't had time to study all the material, but something had to be done to help Hunter. I taped all the photographs of Lettie Lemore and Rudy Lee on a wall. Underneath each picture, I taped arrest reports and newspaper articles. I wrote John Maynard's name on a piece of paper and put it up along with Johnny Stampanato's name. Somehow these individuals fit the narrative of Johnny Stompanto's death and consequentially, Hunter's dismissal. If I could just connect the dots.

I stared at the information until I felt my head would burst. Then I remembered my coat. I went to the closet and rummaged through the pockets, pulling out a key! I kissed it for good luck for I knew what kind of key it was. "Come on, Baby. I think I know how the drugs are being smuggled. Let's find the proof."

26

I knocked on the door.

John Maynard answered, holding his reading glasses in one hand. "Mrs. Reynolds?"

"Josiah. I thought we were on a first name basis."

"Why are you here?"

"May I come in? I'd like to talk with you."

"Sure," he said, standing aside so I could pass. "May I get you something? Coffee or a soft drink?"

"No, thank you."

Maynard showed me into his living room and motioned to a chair. "I'm curious as to why you are here."

"I'll be blunt. I think you are involved in Rudy Lee's demise up to your neck."

Maynard laughed. "That's blunt all right. If that's true, aren't you afraid to be here alone with me?"

"You're not a murderer, but you are causing a great deal of harm to a friend of mine, and I want you to stop."

"You are referring to Dr. Wickliffe."

"Of course, I am."

"What do you think you know?" He leaned back in his chair and chewed on one of the temples of his glasses.

"I know you were stalking Rudy Lee."

Maynard said, "What makes you think so?"

"You were at the crime scene before Dr. Wickliffe and I arrived, and Rudy Lee had only been dead a short time. Even if you had heard something on a police scanner, there was no reason for a crime beat reporter to be there. Murder was never mentioned in the 911 call. Just that an old man had died."

"You forget he had been stabbed in the neck."

"Which was not mentioned in the 911 call. I have a written copy of the call. We both know you stabbed Lee in the neck after you found him dead. You were monitoring Lee with a bug you put inside his house and heard him fall. You went inside his house and found Lee dead."

"If he was already dead, why would I stab him? Makes no sense."

"Anger, Mr. Maynard. Pent-up rage. You had been trailing Lee, hoping to catch him doing something illegal. That's why you had the hi-tech eavesdropping gear. You heard Lee collapse on the floor, rushed in, saw that he was dead, and impulsively grabbed the first thing you could get your hands on. You stabbed him out of pure hatred because of a family member."

Maynard sneered. "I see you have checked up on me. Well, Josiah, this isn't just about one family member. There were two girls walking along the road that night. They were coming home from a movie. My cousin and my sister. Rudy Lee's car jumped the curb and struck them both. My cousin survived. My sister didn't. She was twelve, Mrs. Reynolds. Twelve!"

"Horrible."

"This was just the beginning of what the Lees did to my family. My cousin identified Lee as the driver. Said Lee stumbled out of the car drunk and ran when he saw the carnage. He left those poor girls alone in the dark by the side of the road. Left my sister to die choking on her own blood."

"You must have hated him very much."

"Wouldn't you?"

"I know the rest. The car was registered to Lee, which he claimed was stolen."

"Not to Rutherford Robert Lee but to his father's corporation. His father saved his butt yet again by providing his son with an alibi."

"Lettie Lemore."

"The old man knew of her relationship with his son, and paid Lemore money to cover for him. At that time, Lemore was still known as Pitts."

"So, the police never filed charges."

"As far as they were concerned an unidentified car thief was responsible," Maynard said. "The old man had white-shoe lawyers crawling all over the DA's office threatening lawsuits, forbidding Rudy Lee to cooperate with the police. Then the old man went to our parents and made a deal with them not to pursue the matter. What could they do? Money was needed for my cousin's medical bills and my sister's funeral, so they made a deal with the devil. Rudy's father even threw in a college education for my cousin and me." Maynard laughed bitterly. "My little sister died so I could go to school."

"You left Louisiana after college?"

"I had to get away from the corruption and rot. I tried to put the past behind me, but swore if I ever had the opportunity for revenge, I'd take it. After college, I bummed around the country for a while, learning my craft as a reporter until I finally ended up in Lexington. Been here for ten years. You couldn't believe the shock I felt when I saw Lettie Lemore's picture in the paper as the new go-to girl for the horsey crowd. I knew Rudy Lee would not be far behind. Sure enough, I spotted them together at the Keeneland horse sales."

"What was the true nature of Lemore and Lee's friendship? Were they lovers?"

"At the beginning perhaps, but by the time I caught up with Lee again, he was too old for her. Lemore is still a young woman. Mostly, they were in business together."

"Doing what?"

"Lemore's mother presented herself as a witch and seer in my hometown, but it was a con. She would give a client a bad fortune and say she could remove the curse for a substantial fee."

"People fell for that?"

"Yeah, they paid up, but the mother didn't stop there. Through her fortune telling business, the mother would glean private information from her clients and then resell the information to Rudy's father."

I said, "What a nasty scam."

"Precisely."

"What happened after Rudy beat the rap for the hit and run?"

"The old man was so disgusted that he disowned Rudy. Soon after, Lemore's mother died. Rudy Lee and Lemore teamed up for the same gimmick with Lee arranging 'accidents' if a client didn't take Lemore seriously about the 'curse.' They both were no good and spread misery in their wake. They bled people dry."

"I think Lemore took the occult more seriously than perhaps her mother. What did you glean thumbing through her copy of Liber AL vel Legis?"

Maynard grinned. "I thought that was you scurrying down the sidewalk."

"What makes you think I was at her house?" I protested, unconvincingly. I always squirmed when caught being naughty.

"I saw you. Quit denying it."

It was my turn to grin now. "What gave me away?"

"Your limp. It's slight but still noticeable."

"What did you find in the book?"

"You were right in thinking Lemore took the occult seriously, but the margin notes were about witchcraft. Nothing to do with misdeeds."

"Your plan to connect Lettie Lemore to the hit-and-run driver backfired."

"What do you mean?" Maynard demanded.

"You sent those cryptic texts to a buddy reporter in Las Vegas, knowing he would share them with the police. What you didn't put together was my connection to Lemore and Lee, and it was that connection that got Hunter Wickliffe thrown off the Stompanato case. It's obvious the mentalist mentioned in the emails is Lemore and the henchman is Lee. The message *do as thou wilt* is the keystone to the Liber AL vel Legis. That was Aleister Crowley's mantra—no reins on behavior. *The key has gone to the falls to work for the kingfisher* refers to Lemore coming to Louisville, where the falls of the Ohio River are. Lemore came to Kentucky to do dirty work for the boss man behind the drug running enterprise. I think Lemore is up to her neck in drug smuggling, and she was sent here to somehow implicate Hunter Wickliffe and get him thrown off the case. Any good lawyer can discredit the circumstantial evidence the police have, but Wickliffe's reputation was impeccable, and his testimony was vital to the Stompanato case. He had to go."

Maynard said, "Lemore's been in Kentucky for almost a year. Why not plant drugs in Hunter Wickliffe's car and tip off the police? Seems simpler."

"Because no one would believe Hunter Wickliffe would take drugs. Certainly not the police. Hunter is about as straight an arrow as there is, and the cops know it. Don't you see? They had to do something to make him *want* to quit the case, like threaten his girlfriend."

"Which is you."

I nodded. "Which is me."

Maynard looked downfallen. "I was desperate to get back at the two of them. I knew they were involved with Stompanato's death, but couldn't prove the connection. But as much as I loathed him, I didn't kill Lee. It was as you said. I was monitoring Lee, heard him collapse, and rushed inside to check. I found him dead but I felt cheated. I wanted to cast the killing blow. The stabbing with the scissors was a catharsis."

I reached over and patted his knee. I understood Maynard's deep anger. "Do you know where Lemore is now?"

"Hiding I assume. She can't go back to Las Vegas, and I know she hasn't shown up in Louisiana."

"I think I know where she might be."

Excited, Maynard scooted to the edge of his chair. "Tell me, Mrs. Reynolds."

"Call me Josiah. We've shared so much."

"Please, Josiah."

Grinning, I pulled an object from my pocket and handed it to Maynard, who looked at it curiously. "I found this in Lemore's house. Being from Louisiana, I'm sure you know what this is."

"The ignition key to a boat."

"Mr. Maynard."

"Please call me John. We've shared so much."

"John, feel like a little fishing on the Ohio river? I think we might land a nice big catfish for dinner."

Maynard looked at me with renewed respect. "I'll drive," he said, jumping up to gather his car keys.

I smiled. With good fortune, we would reel in our quarry today. If I were at a craps table right now, I would be throwing sevens. Lady luck was perched on my shoulder. I was sure of it.

27

There were several marinas near Louisville, so we traveled to the closest one near Lettie Lemore's office.

"I don't think a stakeout is the way to go," I complained, sitting in Maynard's parked car where we could see the ski boats and houseboats moored in their slips. "Lemore's in hiding. She's not going to come out for a leisurely stroll. She may not even be here. Lemore may be holed up on a boat at a marina or she could be on her way to Canada."

John argued, "She has to have access to food, electricity, and gas. I think a marina would be the best place for her to hide a boat in plain sight."

"*The Purloined Letter?*"

"You know your Edgar Allan Poe, Josiah. I'm impressed," John said, referring to Poe's short story about a document hidden in plain sight among letters.

"I refuse to sit in a car for hours. You guys can pee in a cup. We gals aren't so lucky."

"What do you suggest?"

"I've got a partial boat registration number. Let's get out and look at the boats. It has to be a boat that's fast and has enough room to hide drug shipments."

"Where did you get the number?"

"Off Rudy Lee's dog which you let out."

"The dog?"

"Yeah, it was on the dog's collar. I could only get a partial. PND 434," I said, looking through binoculars. "Come on. Let's go."

"What happened to the dog?"

"It ended up in a pound, but I tracked down his new owner. The owner repeated what he remembered was on the dog's collar which was a partial boat registration number. I guess Lee was having trouble remembering it. A lot of these boats look alike."

"The dog find a good home?"

"Yep."

"That's good. Why do you think Lee was living in a dump? And where did he get the money to purchase those Standardbreds? Those are not cheap." Maynard wondered aloud, getting out his glasses.

"No doubt the Blue Heron fronted the money for the horses, but I'm sure they won't claim them."

Maynard replied, "Lee's name is on their ownership papers. I checked."

I shrugged as I wasn't really interested. It wasn't my job to tie up every loose end.

"What are we going to do if we find Lemore?"

"Call the police. I'm sure she has some outstanding warrants somewhere. Time for questions is over." I got out of the car and walked down the ramp to the dock looking for the registration numbers painted on the side of the boats. I ruled out pontoons, sailboats, john boats, skiffs, canoes, paddle boats, scows, dinghies, sloops, kayaks, trawlers, catamarans, gondolas, row boats, rafts, and houseboats. I was looking for a cruiser.

Maynard took one side of the marina and I took the other. After twenty minutes of searching, I was on the last row. Several expensive cruisers gently rocked in their slips. I checked the numbers on the sides of the boats. Two of the registration numbers started with PND 434. One was a huge Carver C34 cruiser named The Melissa. The other boat was an older Back Cove 37, which looked like it has seen better days. I spied the name on the hull—Houdini. Gee, that was subtle, but still it could be a coincidence. Both boats were capable of river and lake travel and even though the Houdini needed a paint job and some polishing, she looked seaworthy. I looked for signs of occupancy, but both boats looked forlorn and empty.

A barge sounded its horn while lazily pushing its way toward the Mississippi River. I guess its main stop was St. Louis and to New Orleans from there. The lapping of the waves, the smell of the damp earth, and the sound of the boats bumping into the dock from the swells of the barge made me homesick for the Kentucky River. I thought about taking Lady Elsmere's pontoon boat out for a spin this weekend, but I had to get this ordeal on the Ohio River over first. The only thing to do was to climb aboard the two boats and see if the key fit the ignition.

I checked the first boat again. It certainly looked empty. I crept quietly on board and tiptoed over to the captain's chair. The key went in. I closed my eyes, turning the key. It wouldn't budge. This wasn't the right boat. I sighed with relief.

Several pleasure boats sped up and down the river, making quite a racket. The people on board waved, and I waved back wishing I was enjoying the day with them. I watched them until they disappeared from sight. Determined to get this over, I climbed on board the Houdini and inserted the key into the ignition.

"Don't bother turning it. It's the right key."

I swiveled around and stared at the end of a gun barrel from a Glock. Maybe I should say it was staring at me. "Hello Lettie."

"I saw you slinking around. Looking for me?"

"Good guess."

"They told me you were a nosey goose."

"Who are 'they?'"

"You don't need to know." Lettie motioned me away from the controls. "Sit down on the floor and be quiet."

I did as she commanded. After all, she had a gun

pointed at me. "What are you going to do?"

She untied the lines and started the boat. "We're going for a little ride."

"I didn't come alone. John Maynard is with me."

"Who?"

"The brother of the girl your buddy, Rudy Lee ran down in Louisiana. You surely remember. You provided Lee with an alibi about twenty years ago. You must have been what, eighteen, at the time."

Lettie knitted her brows together. "Oh, now I remember. Louisiana. Poor kid. Wrong place at the wrong time."

"It's her fault Rudy Lee was driving drunk and hit her?"

"Didn't say it was her fault. Just said poor kid." Lettie looked about the dock. "I don't see anyone. I think you are lying. You are here alone."

"Have it your way."

"I always have and I always will."

"You're mighty bold, Lettie. You know the police will charge you as an accessory to murder."

"I haven't talked to Gerry in over a year. I had nothing to do with Stompanato's death."

"And yet, you know about Stompanato and that Gerry Harl is accused of the man's death. There has been no news about Stompanato's death in the media here."

"I still have friends in Las Vegas." She powered the

boat slowly out of its slip.

I could have jumped if it weren't for Lettie holding a gun on me. "If you had nothing to do with Stompanato's death, why are you hiding out? Perhaps you think the people who sent you are cleaning up loose ends like they did with poor Rudy."

"Rudy's death was natural. He died of a heart attack. He was complaining of chest pains for months. I told Rudy to see a doctor. It's his own fault."

"He was stabbed in the neck with a pair of scissors."

Lemore scoffed, "That's not how it's done."

"Oh, really. Not how it's done by a professional? Do tell."

"Shut up."

"Here's something to consider," I countered. "Your boss might be trying to make it look like you killed Rudy Lee. Perhaps you did. After all, Rudy knew all your secrets. The dirty little games you played on innocents." I was throwing mud on the wall and hoping some of it would stick.

"Innocents? You've got to be kidding. There are no innocents in the world. Just big dogs and bigger dogs."

"Eat or be eaten?"

"You got it, lady." I continued to egg Lettie, hurling every conceivable plot at her. I could see I was wearing down her resistance. Was she thinking some of what I babbled was true? And where was Maynard? I hoped he wasn't sitting in his car waiting for me. "Maybe Rudy made a deal with the DA and was going to spill his guts in return for no jail time. Is that why you killed him?"

"I'm telling you Rudy died of a heart attack. He had heart trouble."

"You're lying. I can tell."

Lettie gave me a wolfish grin. "You're right I am."

"Why did you kill him?"

"He got greedy about his cut. Rudy had to go before he squealed."

"He was your partner for years."

Lettie grinned again.

"How did you kill Rudy?"

"It was simple. I used magic. You saw my book of spells."

A chill ran down my spine. I know it's foolish to think so, but I believed her.

Lettie let out the throttle on the boat causing me to fall back against the bench seat. I could tell we were moving east along the south bank of the Ohio River. I also knew there were many miles of tree-lined embankments with no houses or towns coming up where one could dump a body easily. I was helpless though. I couldn't spring up from where I was sitting and jump her. Not with my bad leg and not at my age.

With one hand on the wheel and the other holding the gun, she picked up a circle of braided dock line with the barrel of the gun and tossed the rope at me. "Tie your legs up."

"Like hell I will," I said, grabbing and throwing the line over the side.

Growling like a wounded beast, Lettie stopped the boat and stomped back. "When I tell you to do something, you better do it!" she shrieked, hitting me with the butt of the gun.

Even though I thrust up my hands to protect my head, Lettie got me but good. Stunned, I slumped on the floor. The whimpering sound I heard must have been from me when I tasted my own blood. I felt the boat rushing through the cold river water again. What was it with me and river water? People had tried to kill me at the Kentucky River, the Cumberland River, and now the Ohio River.

How was I going to get out of this mess?

28

"You won't get away with this."

Lettie laughed. "Of course, I will. I get away with everything."

"Do as thou wilt?"

"You found my Book of the Law. I'd like to have it back. Where is it?"

"Not in my possession."

"I can purchase another one. Makes no never mind."

I was woozy and climbed on the bench seat cradling my head. It was a struggle I can tell you.

Lettie hissed, brandishing the gun again, "Sit down on the floor." She stopped the boat planning to beat me unconscious or worse this time. "Now you've asked for it. You stupid cow! You've caused me enough trouble!"

Peeping through my hands, I could see another large barge coming down the river and several pleasure boats passing it, creating a large wake. This was my chance. I knew they would never hear me call for help over the noise of their motors, but perhaps they would see motion. I began jumping up and down while waving my arms. "Help! Help!" I shouted. I don't know why I screamed so. Guess I was desperate.

Spying the other boats and worried about witnesses, Lettie dared not shoot me. They might see the flash from the gun barrel going off, or the loud pop of the gun might penetrate the roars of the boat motors. Full of fury, Lettie rushed me hoping to shove me down before anyone saw. As she made contact, I clutched her waist and pulled Lettie over with me into the freezing waters of the mighty Ohio River.

There is one thing I'm very good at and that is swimming. I prepared myself for the shock of the cold water and knew Lettie would let go as soon as she hit the water. She did. I kicked my way back to the surface losing my shoes in the process. I swam to the boat, pulling myself up the ladder stationed at the boat's stern.

However, Lettie was not a good swimmer. She reached the surface of the water, crying out while sputtering and spewing water from her mouth.

May God forgive me, but for a split second I considered letting her drown. She was a nasty bit of fluff. Lord knows how many lives she had ruined. Lettie Lemore would not be missed in the world, but my Southern Baptist childhood training kicked in. "Don't even think of swimming here," I yelled at her. "If the cold water doesn't kill you, I will if you try to get back in this boat." My Christian kindness only went so far where my life was concerned. I threw a flotation device to Lettie, who splashed her way toward the shoreline.

Shivering and dripping water, I moved the boat into deeper water in case Lettie changed her mind. The boat rocked in the large wake created by the two pleasure boats and the barge, causing me to grab on for dear life or be tossed overboard again. As the rocking lessened, I switched on the boat radio and turned on channel 16. "Mayday! Mayday! Mayday! Help needed on the Houdini. One overboard. Medical attention needed. Mayday! Mayday! Mayday!"

After some crackling on the line, a man answered, "What is the need for medical help? Over."

"Speak up. I can't hear you." I felt my ear where I wore my hearing aid. It was gone. Must have fallen away when I hit the water. "I lost my hearing aid. You must speak up."

"Copy. What is your medical emergency? Over."

I could barely make out what the man was saying. "Hypothermia. I swallowed river water. Another passenger is making her way to the Kentucky shoreline. Lettie Lemore is wanted for questioning in the death of Johnny Stompanato in Las Vegas. I was kidnapped, and my life was threatened. I need help. Over."

There were a few seconds of silence as the dispatcher decided if this was a crank call or if someone was really in need of assistance.

"What is your name? Over."

"Josiah Reynolds. Over."

"Copy. What type of boat? Over."

"A Back Cove 37 painted navy blue. Over."

"Copy. Where is your location? Over."

I looked around, seeing no landmarks. "I don't know. East of Louisville. Past Sidwell's Marina. There are no buildings that I can see. Just woodlands. I'm stationed in the middle of the river on the Houdini. Over."

"Look at your GPS navigational screen. It should be above the boat's steering wheel. What do the coordinates say? Over."

I didn't reply as I passed out. With all my strength and energy depleted, I didn't come to until the Coast Guard Auxiliary paramedics jumped on board the Houdini.

Ah, the cavalry had arrived.

29

The hospital let me go that very evening, instructing me to rest while taking plenty of fluids. Ah, duh.

Maynard escorted me from the emergency room to his car, whereupon we were met by Detective Drake and his counterpart in the Louisville police. Despite our pleas that we needed rest and food, Maynard and I were separated and whisked away to the nearest police station.

I was stuck in a mean little interrogation room for over an hour until Drake and two other people crowded into the room.

Drake spoke into a camera set up for the interview. "Let the record show that I am Detective Drake from the Lexington Police Department, and my associate is Detective Linda Culbert from the Kentucky State Police."

"Who are you?" I asked the tall man in uniform.

"Special Agent Tull from the CGIS."

"Speak up, please. I lost my hearing aid when I went

into the water and can't hear."

Agent Tull repeated that he was from the CGIS. "Can you hear me now?"

I nodded. "The Coast Guard Investigative Service. Well. Well. I take it you found drugs on the Houdini."

Tull answered, "Yes, ma'am, we did."

Drake shot Tull a nasty look.

"Did you apprehend Lettie Lemore?" I asked.

Culbert smiled. "It took us a few hours, but we got her."

"Is she here?"

"Yes, and she is spinning quite a yarn," Drake said, speaking slowly like I was a half-wit.

"I would imagine. She's a consummate liar. Is she spinning tales about me?"

Drake said, "Doesn't look good for you."

"And you are about to wet your pants thinking you've got something on me," I countered.

Drake's face flushed while Tull managed a small smile before dismissing it.

"Josiah, you should take this very seriously," Detective Culbert said.

"Okay, Linda. What are the charges?"

"Obstruction for one. Tampering with evidence for a second. Breaking and entering for a third. Possible kidnapping. Transportation of illegal drugs. Stealing a vessel. Aggravated assault." Drake took a breath. "That's quite a list, even for you."

"Listen, fellows. Speak up. I can hear only half of what you are saying. I need some dry clothes, a meal, and a bed. If not, you are going to have to take me back to the hospital because I'm crashing. Now the four of us know that if I don't get these things, and my health goes south, any defense attorney, worth her salt, will get my testimony thrown out in court. I'll be more than happy to give a complete statement tomorrow, but I'll leave you with this. I did not kidnap Lettie Lemore, have anything to do with the death of Rutherford Robert Lee, or partake in any drug smuggling scheme. Lettie Lemore kidnapped me with the intention of shooting me and throwing my body into the Ohio River when I confronted her about the Johnny Stompanato case and drug smuggling for the Blue Heron Casino. That's all I have to say for now. I'll see the three of you at ten tomorrow morning. Now if one of you would be so kind as to call me a cab and direct me to the nearest hotel with room service." I stood and walked out of the room.

Determined to keep me in town, Detective Culbert had an officer drive me to a mall where she ran in and purchased a casual outfit for me and then drove me to a hotel. I thanked the officer profusely and when I entered the hotel, the management was already expecting me. The first thing I did was call my lawyer, Shaneika Mary Todd. After a brief conversation with her, I ordered room service, made a call to Charles letting him know where I was and to take care of my animals, changed out of my grimy clothes, took a hot shower, ate, watched a little silly TV before falling asleep.

The next morning Shaneika picked me up at the hotel and drove me to the police station where Detective Culbert and Special Agent Tull took my statement. Drake had gone back to Lexington. I told my story as succinctly as possible but leaving out that I had searched Lemore's house, taken the boat key, and seen Maynard there. I hope he had done the same for me.

"Why did you and Maynard go to the marina?" Detective Culbert asked.

"Maynard wanted to expose Lemore for the false alibi she gave Lee for the death of his sister. I wanted Lemore to confess to having instigated an attack on me at Wickliffe Manor."

Tull said, "I can see why Maynard wanted to be involved, but I don't see how you teaming up with him would prove anything about Lee and the tree limb incident."

"It was a hunch."

"What made you think of looking for Lettie Lemore at a marina?"

"She's from southern Louisiana. Every one is boat crazy there and seemed only natural."

"Not buying it, Mrs. Reynolds," Culbert said. She had learned her lesson calling me by my first name.

"It seemed logical. Everyone assumes all drug

shipments travel up I-75 through Lexington, but no one was singing. Right? You never got any tips about it. So the drugs had to be smuggled another way. Then I thought if Lettie Lemore was catering to the horsey set, why was she based in Louisville? The horses are in Lexington. Then I see the river route, and it just clicked in my head. Louisville sits right on the Ohio River and is close to the Mississippi River."

Tull said, "Lemore said you had a spare boat key for the Houdini when you came on board. The only place you could have gotten it was from her house."

"I haven't the foggiest idea what Lemore's talking about," I lied. "Lemore is a career criminal. She'll say anything to save her own neck." Was my nose getting bigger? I was sure telling whoppers.

"We have video of you going into her house," Detective Culbert said.

"You may have a tape of someone going into her house, but it wasn't me." If they really had a surveillance tape, Culbert and Tull would have mentioned point of entry. I was calling their bluff. "Are you checking on her relationship with Gerry Harl?"

"We are checking on everything," Culbert said.

Shaneika spoke up. "As you can see from the medical report, Mrs. Reynolds suffered greatly at the hands of Lettie Lemore. A blow to the head, loss of her hearing aid, a gash on her lips, scratches and bruises all over her body, not to mention swallowing contaminated river water. It is plain to see my client is the victim of a vicious assault. She is on antibiotics and is scheduled for a MRI tomorrow."

"Mrs. Reynolds claims she was hit with the butt of a gun. We found no such weapon," Special Agent Tull said.

"That's because it fell into the river when we both went over the side of the boat during the struggle," I sputtered.

"Lemore says you pushed her into the river," Detective Culbert said.

"The woman was trying to kill me!"

Shaneika asked, "Are you going to charge my client?"

Culbert closed a file. "Not at this time."

"I demand to know if my client is considered a witness or a suspect."

Culbert and Tull glanced at each other.

"I thought so." Shaneika stood and handed them both a business card. "From now on, you will speak to me first where it might concern Mrs. Reynolds. Good day to you."

I rose and thanked my lucky stars for Shaneika Mary Todd. She had gotten me out of another jam.

Now I had to go home and face Hunter. I'm not sure he would be happy with my interference. Oh, I was sure he'd be unhappy. That was one jam Shaneika couldn't help me with—my love life.

Did I still have one?

30

I didn't see Hunter for weeks, which stretched into a month. Spring was in full bloom and the bees were going berserk trying to collect all the nectar from dandelions sprouting in glorious yellow on my farm. Shaneika called me and said Hunter was being investigated by both the Las Vegas police and the DEA for collusion. He would not be in contact until after the law enforcement agencies made their final recommendations. I was to talk to them as well, and Shaneika set up the appointments. I felt terrible. If I hadn't suggested to Rudy Lee to lease out Hunter's farm, this whole chain of events would never have happened.

Matt told me to shove those thoughts out of my head. He claimed Lee and Lemore would have conspired to get to Hunter somehow. It was their plan all along to discredit Hunter. They knew the evidence against Gerry Harl would never stand up in court with a clever lawyer at his side if Hunter never testified.

I went about my business and worked. The hens

were laying now, so I purchased sixteen more. I was now in the egg business and starting to pick up customers for them. Franklin was right about the profit margin. In the early weeks, I could only muster eight to ten cartons which was barely enough to pay for the gas to the market, but as the hens began laying more and more, I was edging toward a profit. Maybe.

My truce with the fox was a delicate balance. I know she tried to get into the coop every once in a while, but the electric fence kept her at bay. I don't know why I thought the fox was female, but she acted female. You know what I mean?

Baby did his part to keep the fox away, and I know he disapproved of me leaving food out for it. Since coyotes had moved into the Bluegrass, foxes had almost become a thing of the past. I wanted to help the fox maintain her territory. I loved her red coat with white markings. She was quite stunning, but like Hunter, I didn't see her for weeks, that is, until she showed herself briefly with her three kits—lovely little furballs traipsing after their mother while I was working the bees. I think she was trying to tell me she was all right and not to worry.

But I did, especially if I would not have Hunter after this debacle was over.

The simple truth was I didn't want to grow old alone.

31

Ever have a day where everything goes right? All the traffic lights are green, it doesn't rain, the IRS letter you receive with shaking hands states a mistake was made in your favor, birds sing as you pass by, you receive compliments on your new hairdo, and strange dogs don't bark, but wag their tails in delight at the sight of you. We have maybe five days like this in our life. I was having a day like that.

Renata Gomez gave me a call. My van was ready. I was ecstatic, so I rushed over to the equipment shop. Renata had a tarp over the van. "Stand right here," she said, centering me in front of the van. "I think this is going to blow your mind." She tore off the tarp and waited for my reaction.

I couldn't believe my VW van. It had a new paint job with a turquoise underbody and a white top with the rust and corrosion repaired. All the windows had been replaced including the two split windshields, and the van boasted four new white wall tires that highlighted the polished chrome. "I told you to get her running. Not restore her." I was angry. So angry. How was I going to pay for this?

Renata's face fell. "She does run. Purrs like a kitten just like I promised. I replaced the battery. She's got all new hoses, plugs, distributor—the works. You will pay for that work. As for the cosmetics, it was paid for by a Hunter Wickliffe. He left you a letter in the front seat. Here's the key." She handed the key to me and walked off.

My perfect day was just blown. The letter was probably a Dear Jane letter, the third one I've gotten in life. Hunter just wanted to soften the blow with refurbishing the van. With a heavy heart, I opened the driver's door and climbed in, looking about. All the upholstery had been replaced giving the van that new car smell. It was heavenly.

Seeing a letter addressed to me on the dashboard, I put it on the passenger's seat. I didn't want to deal with it right now. I slowly turned the key. The van started right up and I drove her home where I parked her in front of the Butterfly. I sat in the van for a long time remembering my shared life with it. Brannon and I camped with it after we were first married. I took Asa took school in it. I hauled beehives and equipment around the farm in it. I lugged my honey to the farmers market in it. Matt and I went sightseeing in it. So many wonderful memories. So much time had passed.

Brannon was dead. Asa was all grown up. Matt was a
father now. The only consistent thing in my life were
the honeybees. Thank God for them.

Gathering up my courage, I opened the letter with
great trepidation.

Dearest Josiah,

*I fear you have been exposed to awful stress because of my
vocation. I never meant for you to be subjected to the
ugliness of my job. It is dark and brutish work. The only
way I can apologize is doing something nice for you.
Words do not suffice. I know you love this old van, and
Franklin said you were having it looked at. Please allow
me to have it smarted up. When you drive it, think of me
for I shall be gone for quite some time.*

*My name has been cleared and I am currently in Las
Vegas, where the DA is having me testify at Gerry
Harl's trial. Through me, the DA and the police hope to
prove the connection between Lettie Lemore, Gerry Harl,
and The Blue Heron Casino in their attempts to discredit
me as a consultant. I am testifying as a witness for the
prosecution and not as an employee.*

*As for Rudy Lee, his death is still inconclusive. It
will never be known if he was murdered or died of natural
causes. Lettie Lemore is not talking except to say she
killed him with a magic spell. I think she is going after
the insanity plea. Still defiant as ever, she will not make
a deal with the DA. I guess she fears her drug bosses*

more than prison. Personally, I think Lee was bumped off by the cartel, but his case will remain inconclusive for now.

Your buddy, John Maynard, is here, and I see him every day in the courtroom. He has quit Lexington and taken a job with the local rag. He speaks highly of you. Thought I would pass the compliment along.

After Las Vegas, I am flying to Seattle to look at a crime scene, and after that to Oklahoma City. Franklin is closing up Wickliffe Manor for me and seeing to the property. The horses have already been sold, which is how I could afford the van restoration.

Please wait for me, my darling. As soon as I get back on my feet financially, I will be home to you with open arms. Until then, I will be living out of a suitcase. Enjoy the van. I will call first chance I get.

Forever, Hunter

I went home and threw my pain pills off the cliff as it began to rain.

You're not done yet!
Read On For An Exciting Bonus Chapter
DEATH BY SHOCK

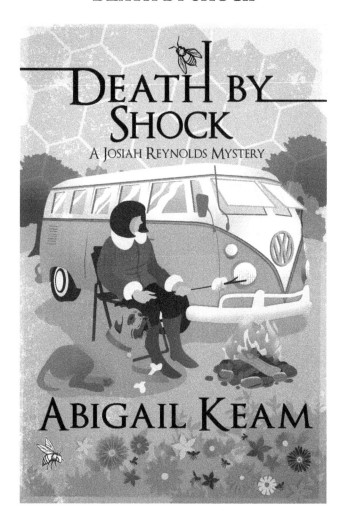

1

"Watch what you're doing!" Shaneika snapped.

"Move then," I hissed back.

Shaneika and I were stuck like two peas in a pod falling over each other in a muddy trench.

Since Comanche had retired from horse racing and was now standing at stud, Shaneika had extra time and decided to try her hand at archaeology. As an enthusiastic amateur historian, archaeology was the next logical step for her. She joined the Daniel Boone Archaeological Society and assisted at digs. Shaneika decided her involvement meant that I was involved as well. The Society needed volunteers to dig an area to the west of Fort Boonesborough where freestanding cabins had stood, so Shaneika signed me up.

How could I refuse? As my attorney, Shaneika had saved my tush many times. Now I was pushing *her* tush out of the way. "You broke the string," I complained, glaring at the snapped filament lying limp on the ground. The university's archaeologists had carefully plotted out a grid of squares for us to excavate, and now one entire strand was on the ground.

"I'll put it back. No need to get your panties in a wad." Shaneika climbed out of our little ditch and pulled the string taut again. "There! Good as new, Miss Fussbucket."

I complained, "I don't understand why we are doing this."

"My ancestor, John Todd, came to Kentucky in 1775. His brothers, Levi and Robert Todd, followed."

"I know that, Shaneika. You crow about it often enough."

"I thought you were descended from Levi Todd," Heather said, putting dirt which needed to be sifted through a screen into a bucket.

"And John Todd didn't even come to Boonesborough. He went to Logan's Station," I reminded Shaneika.

"Todd came through here. He just didn't stay here. I bring him up because of his connection to Daniel Boone. Did you know that John Todd was appointed by the one and only 'give me liberty or give me death' Patrick Henry in 1778 as Lt. Commander of Illinois, and that he represented Kentucky in the General Assembly of Virginia in 1778? He introduced bills to emancipate slaves and set aside land for educational purposes."

"That's rich coming from a family of slave owners," I said.

Shaneika pursed her lips in irritation. She was proud of her heritage and connection to her namesake Mary Todd Lincoln and thus to Abraham Lincoln.

Shaneika, her cousin Heather, and I were at Fort Boonesborough trying to locate the fort's original garbage pit which meant their former outhouse location. Since Hunter was still away and I was trying to wean myself off pain medication, I thought it sounded like a fun adventure. Oh, how stupid can one person be?

It had drizzled the night before, and all the trenches the archaeologists had dug were muddy. It was chilly, the porta potty wasn't installed until late in the morning, and the food truck failed to arrive. I was wet, hungry, and aggravated.

Heather Warfield cackled. "You two fight like an old married couple."

I glanced over at Heather, who was thirty-nine and single, financially independent, lived with two rescue cats, and worked in an animal shelter. She was Rubenesque with ivory skin, long brown hair clipped up into a pony tail, large dark expressive eyes that were nearsighted, and a small mouth. Heather's vocabulary spoke of an extensive education, as she had graduated with degrees in political science and economics. So why was Heather working at an animal shelter and not in her fields of expertise? Was it because she was shy and unassuming? I didn't inquire as that would be uncouth, but that wouldn't stop me from asking Shaneika when we were alone. Yep, I'm a nosey cuss.

It was also evident Heather was a huge UK basketball fan from her UK sweatshirt and UK decals on her sunglasses and watch band. She was also a relative of Shaneika's. They were distant cousins.

The Warfields and the Todds were part of the first wave of European pioneers who lived in the Bluegrass and thus accumulated a fortune through land acquisition and hemp crops. Dr. Elisha Warfield dabbled in horse racing and bred the stallion, Lexington, or Big Lex as the locals called him. You see pictures all over the area of Big Lex, who is colored blue. It gives the tourists pause. Why is the horse portrayed as blue? Folklore has it that the ghost of a "blue" Big Lex can be seen grazing in pastures. The apparition acquired its hue from all the bluegrass he has consumed. Kentucky bluegrass has a bluish tint when allowed to grow to full height, which is why the area around Lexington is called the Bluegrass. Quaint story, huh!

Of course, the Warfields and the Todds intermarried with the other pioneer families as did most of the first European families in this area, so Heather and Shaneika have common ancestors. I studied both of them as I carefully trowelled away thin layers of dirt in our pit.

One of the cousins was pale as a Junco's white underbelly, and the other cousin had light copper-colored skin. Heather was shy and introverted while Shaneika was a lioness and, for my money, the best criminal lawyer in the state of Kentucky. Love, hate, devotion, cruelty, racism, classism, slavery, elitism, heartbreak, repression, and struggle had been bound together in a sacred dance throughout Kentucky history, culminating in Shaneika and Heather, polar opposites, but related by blood and history. They were two women who had come to terms with the sins and accomplishments of their ancestors, embracing their shared past.

That's why we were at Fort Boonesborough sifting through mud with a trowel and a paint brush. Shaneika knew her European ancestors' line of descent, but there were gaps with her African heritage. Shaneika wanted to close those gaps and pass the information on to her son, Lincoln.

In Shaneika's office is a letter from Abraham Lincoln to George Rogers Clark Todd (Mary Todd Lincoln's brother), a Confederate officer's sword, daguerreotypes of black women washing at Camp Nelson (a Union military post during the Civil War and now a military cemetery), and other various Civil War artifacts which she claims are family heirlooms. Though Shaneika won't tell me how exactly she is descended from the Todd family, I know I will drag it out of her one day. At the moment, however, moisture from the muck I knelt in was seeping through my jeans causing me to complain, "I'm going back to the van and change. My pants are getting soaked."

"Boo hoo," Shaneika said, sneering as she plucked a pottery shard from the dirt caked on her trowel. "If you change, you'll get those pants filthy as well." She motioned to the field photographer to photograph the find and then she cataloged it.

I grumbled, "This is crazy. We're not finding anything but broken clay pipe stems and animal bone fragments."

"Let's hope they're animals and not my ancestors," Heather teased. She and Shaneika grinned at each other. "You know the settlers at Jamestown, Virginia resorted to cannibalism."

"Lovely," I replied.

Shaneika said, "Did you know my ancestor John Todd commanded a group of 182 frontiersmen against the British and Shawnee in retaliation for an attack on Bryan Station?"

"Here we go again about John Todd," I murmured.

"What was that?" Shaneika asked.

I said in a louder voice, "We all know about the Battle of Blue Licks in 1782, which is considered the last battle of the Revolutionary War even though the war was officially over." I put another clay pipe stem into a bag and marked it on my grid paper. The information marked on the paper would later be put into a computer.

"I bring it up because Daniel Boone accompanied

John Todd and wanted to wait for reinforcements before engaging the enemy."

Heather looked at Shaneika. "I'm not familiar with this story. Just bits and pieces. What happened then?"

"Some hothead named Hugh McGary accused the men of being cowards and got them riled up, so they attacked. Daniel Boone was remembered to have said, 'We are all slaughtered men now.'"

I said, "A bunch of testosterone driven men who got themselves and their kinfolk dead in my opinion. Of course, Hugh McGary survived. He just had everyone else killed."

Shaneika ignored me and continued regaling us with the Battle of Blue Licks. "Boone was right. It was a trap and they should have waited for reinforcements which were a day away. Not only was John Todd killed, but several members of the Boone family as well, including Daniel Boone's son, Israel. Daniel Boone caught a riderless horse and tried to give it to his son. The story goes that Israel was hesitant to leave his father and in those few seconds was shot to death. Boone then jumped on the horse and rode to safety. Boone had to come back days later to reclaim his son's body and take him to Boone's Station to be buried. There's a stone memorial to Israel Boone still standing. In a battle that lasted less than ten minutes, seventy-two frontiersmen were dead and eleven captured by the Shawnee and the British force."

"Israel's not buried here at Fort Boonesborough?" Heather asked, looking up from her digging.

"I thought Israel was buried at the battle site," I said.

Shaneika said, "No, he's buried at Boone's Station. There's nothing there anymore, but a stone memorial and a historical marker. John Todd is buried in a common grave at the battle site. There is a memorial to all the men who died."

"I find Daniel Boone a controversial figure," Heather said. "Wasn't he adopted by the Shawnee at one point and rumored to have had a Shawnee wife?"

"Some historians believe that he was adopted by the great Shawnee chief, Blackfish, himself. As for a Shawnee wife, who knows? Probably."

I looked at Heather. "I thought you knew all this."

Heather replied, "I know very little about the frontiersmen's period, except for my family. I like to concentrate on history from 1860 through the Reconstruction period."

"Oh," I said. "Well then you might not know that Daniel Boone was not the only one playing around. There is speculation that Edward Boone, Daniel's brother, got Rebecca Boone pregnant while Daniel was on a two year long hunt. Of course, I don't blame Rebecca. She thought Daniel was dead. It's just that Edward Boone was married to her sister Martha, and they were both pregnant around the same time."

"Yikes," Heather said, laughing. "Messy. I wonder what those family get-togethers were like. What did Daniel Boone say when he got back and found a wee babe in the crib?"

"Not much. It seemed Daniel Boone accepted some of the responsibility since he was away for so long and recognized the child as his own. In fact, Jemima was considered his favorite child."

Heather asked, "Is this the scandal that caused Boone to have a falling out with Boonesborough?"

"No, that was due to the aftermath of the Great Siege of Boonesborough. That story had to do with the need for salt from Blue Licks. Boone was considered a Tory and was later court-martialed for treason, but he was acquitted. The trial left Boone so bitter, he moved to his son's small community named Boone's Station near Athens. The Battle of Blue Licks happened four years later than the Great Siege."

"Sounds like Blue Licks was not a lucky place for the Boones," Heather commented.

"I believe I was speaking about my illustrious ancestor, John Todd when I was so rudely interrupted," Shaneika complained, bumping me with her elbow.

"Sorry," I said, looking sheepish. "I do have a tendency to go on."

Looking smug at my apology, Shaneika continued, "As I was saying, seventy-two frontiersmen were killed at the Battle of Blue Licks including John Todd. He was thirty-two years old."

"My gosh, that is young," I said. "And he was a colonel?"

Shaneika said, "Life expectancy was short, so they got on with the business of living. Daniel Boone's daughter, Susannah, was fourteen when she married. Many think she had the first white baby in Kentucky."

"You said 'white baby.' I guess that means something," I alleged.

"The first non-indigenous baby to be born in Kentucky is thought to have been Frederick, a baby born to Dolly, a slave, and her master Richard Callaway in 1775."

"That doesn't sound like a pleasant story," Heather said, looking at Shaneika in dismay. "Do you think they loved each other?"

Shaneika snorted, "For God's sake, get real, Heather. You know what that relationship was about."

I didn't comment because sex between slave owners and slaves was a touchy subject. I didn't like the thought of those poor women's plight or any woman in sexual jeopardy. As a female, it made me uncomfortable. Made me want to take a gun and shoot some man.

The three of us returned to our work, reflecting quietly on the hardships women endured in pioneer life—hardships women have always endured.

"A pipe bowl this time. Did these men do nothing but smoke? And where did they get the tobacco? I haven't read any accounts of tobacco being grown at Fort Boonesborough," I sputtered, sticking the bowl stem in another bag.

Shaneika said, "The women smoked as well. I think when they ran out of tobacco, they smoked other plants. Besides sex and eating, what pleasures did these people have? There was no TV. No restaurants. No spas. No sports. No movies. No theater. No concerts. Not even the simple pleasures of bathing. The women and children couldn't even go outside the fort for a walk. I read somewhere that a woman recounted for a historian that as a child, her mother wouldn't let her leave the fort for over two years because it was too dangerous. Two years!"

"If you put it that way, I guess smoking was one of the few enjoyments they had to counteract the endless work and stress," I said, reaching back and feeling the back of my pants. "Oh, the moisture is soaking through to my panties now. Ugh."

"You sure it's not you losing control?" Shaneika teased.

"I'm not there yet, but give me a few years. As one gets older, all the orifices loosen. Just you wait. Your turn will come."

Heather asked, "If you don't like to excavate, Josiah, why did you come?"

"Josiah is detoxing from pain medication while Hunter is away," Shaneika shot back.

"Is Hunter your gentleman friend, Josiah?" Heather asked, grinning at me. "How serious is your relationship? Come on. Spill it."

"Gee, thanks, Shaneika. I don't think the people over in the next county heard you imply that I am a drug addict," I hissed back, resisting the urge to thump Shaneika on her newly shaved head or pull out one of her large hoop earrings, this being her current look. She was the only woman I knew who changed hairstyles like some women change purses.

"Are you really addicted to drugs?" Heather asked, her large eyes widening.

Wiggling her eyebrows, Shaneika added, "Pain medication."

I replied, "Let's say I'm trying to improve my health and leave it at that." Taking a breather, I looked around. "Boy, I'd really like a drink right now."

"True junkie talk. One drug substituting for another."

"You know, Shaneika, I'm gonna punch your self-righteous snout right in your nose."

Shaneika turned and stared at me. "That makes no sense, Josiah. A snout *is* a nose."

"You know what I mean."

"You better not be having a stroke, because I'm not gonna drag your white fanny out of this pit."

"Yeah?"

"Yeah."

"Make me."

"Girls! Ladies! Behave!" Heather insisted. "Decorum at all times when in public."

Shaneika and I both turned to Heather and yelled, "SHUT UP!"

Heather's face turned crimson.

Ashamed that we had hurt Heather's feelings, I said, "Don't worry, Heather. No one is looking at us. Everyone is staring at the twins." I was referring to the two fabulous women occupying the pit on the other side of the site. They were the Dane twins, both identical with pale skin, startlingly light blue eyes, athletic figures, and ebony hair with a shock of gray at their widow peaks. I couldn't tell if the gray shock was natural or artificial. As I stated before, they were identical. I could never tell them apart.

"What's their story again?" Shaneika asked.

I replied, "I know them well enough to say hello and that's it. I met them once through Lady Elsmere at one of her parties. I doubt they would remember me."

Heather eagerly glanced about to see if anyone was listening to our conversation. Seeing that everyone seemed intent upon their work, she spoke in a stage whisper, "The Dane twins are from Baltimore, and their father was an industrialist who worked for the Navy. Apparently, he supplied them with some type of screw they needed and made a fortune. Of course, that was years back. These girls are from his second marriage late in life."

"They are hardly girls," Shaneika commented, looking at them from the corner of her eye. "More like late thirties or early forties."

"They are thirty-five," Heather said.

I said, "Hmm. They look older."

"They partied very hard when young, and tragedy has followed them throughout their lives," Heather explained. "Haven't you heard of the Dane curse?"

"It's a novel by Dashiell Hammett."

"No, Josiah, this is for real," Heather insisted.

"Like how?" I asked, suddenly interested. Talk of curses always fascinated me.

"Both wives of Mr. Dane died from accidents. The first Mrs. Dane died in a skiing accident. She collided with a tree."

"Holy moly, that's harsh," Shaneika said.

"The second Mrs. Dane died in a car accident when her chauffeur drove off a cliff. There were rumors the two were involved, and the 'accident' was really a murder/suicide when she refused to leave old man Dane."

"Wow," I said.

"Double wow," Shaneika said, putting down her trowel and staring at the Dane women.

I slapped her foot. "You're ogling."

Shaneika countered, "I'm not ogling. I'm studying them."

"You're gawking."

"They might need a sharp lawyer for their legal team. I'm going over there and hand them my card." Shaneika stared at my astonished face. "Well, you never know. Josiah, since you know them, you must introduce me to them."

"Like I told you, I've met them once for a brief introduction. I hardly call that knowing them. Not only can I not tell them apart, I don't remember their names."

"It's Magda and Maja," Heather offered, "but the story doesn't end with the second Mrs. Dane's death."

"There's more?" I asked.

"Quite a bit, I'm afraid," Heather said. "Before old man Dane died, he discovered one of his adult children from his first marriage was embezzling from the family firm, and he disinherited him. Ultimately the embezzler died from a drug overdose. Apparent suicide."

"How many children did Mr. Dane have in all?" Shaneika asked.

Looking smug, Heather replied, "Five. One died in infancy."

"Another whammy," Shaneika commented.

"How do you know all of this, Heather?" I asked, bagging more animal bones before marking their location on a grid survey. I motioned for a volunteer to carry the bones away for analysis.

"I read the *New York Times* and the *Wall Street Jour-*

nal. The Dane family has been written about ad nauseam."

"I never heard of the family before meeting the twins," I said. "I don't know how I could have missed all this drama. It's right up my alley."

"I'm not finished," Heather said.

Shaneika exclaimed. "There's more?"

"Yeah, a real cliffhanger."

"Ugh, Heather, enough with the references to cliffs, please," I complained.

"Sorry, Josiah. I forget you fell off a cliff yourself."

I remarked, "My stomach is turning."

"You gotta hear this though. It turned out that old man Dane disinherited all of his children, except for Magda, the older of the twins."

Shaneika asked, "He did this why?"

"Magda has a real knack for business, and he felt she would preserve the family business and fortune. He was right. The Dane brand has expanded under her leadership—tech companies, facial recognition software, robotic firms—stuff to do with national security."

"Even though Magda expanded the company, it would still piss me off if I were Maja," Shaneika offered.

I asked, "What about the other Dane offspring?"

"The older sister from the first marriage keeps out of the limelight. She has a cottage on Martha's Vineyard."

"What's her name?" I asked.

"Margot, I think," Heather replied, staring at the twins.

Shaneika said, "Magda controls her siblings because she holds the family purse strings. That's what I would do to make them behave and keep them at arms length."

"And Maja?" I asked, amused that Heather seemed to be a crime buff.

"She lives in the guest house on the family estate in Baltimore, where the family firm is still located. I think they live on an island in the bay."

Shaneika asked, "Why not inside the family home?"

"Magda lives there with her husband, Gavin McCloud."

I clucked, "Imagine having your own island in Chesapeake Bay."

Shaneika turned to me. "Sounds similar to the Lee case you were involved in a few months back. By the way, is Hunter still working on that case?"

"He called the other night and said that Rudy Lee's partner in crime, Lettie Lemore pleaded guilty to illegal drug distribution and evidence tampering in a plea deal. The DA dropped the charge for conspiracy to commit murder in the death of Johnny Stompanato, but she still refused to talk about Lee. We might never know how Lee really died."

"What are you two talking about?" Heather asked.

"An acquaintance of Josiah's who died a month or so ago. That's all."

Heather looked confused. "You must tell me, Jo. I didn't read about it in the paper."

"There was a little article about the man's death in the paper. The reporter has since quit Lexington and relocated to Las Vegas."

"Was it murder?"

"Don't know. Death was ruled inconclusive."

Heather said, "I don't know how you do it, Josiah. You keep your cool so. I would just fall apart seeing a dead body. I really would. And the confrontations you have had with murderers. I would freeze. I know I would. You know I keep up with you in the papers. You've got a reputation for solving murders. I confess I'm quite a fan." She leaned over in a conspiratorial fashion. "What are the details of your friend's death? Leave nothing out."

"He wasn't my friend, but I'll tell you about it another time, Heather. I see the food truck has arrived. I'm going to get something."

I needed to eat. I was getting the shakes from weaning myself off so much pain medication. Food helped with the withdrawal—mainly booze and chocolate, the important food groups.

Just breathe, Josiah, I told myself. *Just breathe. You'll be all right.*

Books By Abigail Keam

Death By A HoneyBee I
Death By Drowning II
Death By Bridle III
Death By Bourbon IV
Death By Lotto V
Death By Chocolate VI
Death By Haunting VII
Death By Derby VIII
Death By Design IX
Death By Malice X
Death By Drama XI
Death By Stalking XII
Death By Deceit XIII
Death By Magic XIV
Death By Shock XV

The Mona Moon Mystery Series
Murder Under A Blue Moon I
Murder Under A Blood Moon II
Murder Under A Bad Moon III
Murder Under A Silver Moon IV
Murder Under A Wolf Moon V
Murder Under A Black Moon VI
Murder Under A Full Moon VII
Murder Under A New Moon VIII

About The Author

Hi, I'm Abigail Keam. I write the award-winning *Josiah Reynolds Mystery Series* and the *Mona Moon 1930s Mystery Series*. In addition, I write *The Princess Maura Tales* (Epic Fantasy) and the *Last Chance For Love Series* (Sweet Romance).

I am a professional beekeeper and have won awards for my honey from the Kentucky State Fair. I live in a metal house with my husband and various critters on a cliff overlooking the Kentucky River. I would love to hear from you, so please contact me. Until we meet again, dear friend, happy reading!

You can purchase books directly from my website: www.abigailkeam.com

CPSIA information can be obtained
at www.ICGtesting.com
Printed in the USA
LVHW042134150223
739643LV00015B/164

9 781953 478009